The Night Before
by
David Fulmer

To Joanne
Grazie!
Best to you
[signature]
Xmas 2012

A Bang Bang Lulu Edition

First Print Edition

Copyright © 2012 by David Fulmer

All rights reserved. No part of this publication may be reproduced or transmitted in any form or by any means, electrical or mechanical, including photocopy, recording, or any information storage and retrieval system, without written permission from the author. Requests for permission may be submitted online at mail@bang-bang-lulu.com.

www.bang-bang-lulu.com

Publisher-Supplied Cataloging-in-Publication Data
Fulmer, David.
The night before / David Fulmer. — 1st ed.
1. Christmas-Fiction. I. Title.
ISBN: 978-0-9886105-0-7

Cover Photo:
"Central Moravian Steeple at Sunset"
by Dana Grubb
Used by Permission

Published in the United States of America

Also by David Fulmer

Lost River

The Blue Door

The Dying Crapshooter's Blues

Rampart Street

The Fall

Jass

Chasing the Devil's Tail

*To Sansanee, for making this –
and so much more – possible.*

THE STORM BEGAN late in the afternoon after the sky had darkened from crystal blue to cobalt, delivering snow on Christmas Eve for the first time in seven years. The fat, pillowy flakes descending in a slow swirl brought gentle memories to Joe Kelly's mind, faded pictures from the happiest part of his childhood. It was one blessing atop another, and about damned time.

Facing yet another holiday season with pockets on empty, he had been living in dread of Mariel's wrath. She could make it hard on him and the kids by staying angry right into the New Year. Except this time around, he had a little surprise that would change all that.

Actually, not so little. After the better part of a decade scratching his way up a glass mountain, and with just twelve days before Christmas, his agent had called from New York with a breathless bulletin that a certain A-list actor had stumbled upon his first novel, loved it, and promptly made an offer to option it. Joe could hear the wonder in her voice; she couldn't believe it, either. The amount of money quoted, though not stupendous, caused his breath to come short.

After they clicked off, he reeled around the house, sloppy drunk without having touched a drop, working his brain to process news that was edging on fabulous. He grabbed the phone three times to call Mariel, then snapped it shut again. It was no time for an ordinary *Oh, by the way, honey...* And though bursting to shout the news from the Eastborough rooftops, over the next days he accepted, signed, and FedEx'd a contract back to California, all without uttering a word to anyone except his old friend Billy, who took his turn at stunned silence before whooping like a redneck at a rodeo.

Once the initial rush had passed, Joe fretted himself into a funk until his agent called to confirm that the actor's manager had done as promised and sent an advance, eighty-five percent of which flew into hiding in the savings account, inflating the balance in an electronic banking instant from a straggling three to a robust five figures. When he visited the ATM to check on the deposit, the little slip of paper appeared with the zeroes lined up like fat, sassy eggs.

Still not quite believing the U-turn in his fortunes,

he went inside and withdrew fifty new hundred-dollar bills. The teller counted the stack into his hand and wished him a happy holiday.

The cash rested in his inside pocket as he drove across town. By the time he reached Gateway Mall, the snow was laying and he noticed the cheer on the faces of his fellow shoppers. The weatherman had announced that it would continue on and off through the night, and everyone was giddy.

Joe burst in from the storm, attacking the stores like the American consumer he'd never been, running amok through Target, Boscov's, and Toys"R"Us, blowing a fistful of his crisp hundreds on gifts for the wife and kids. He worked his way down his list, bought some more, and then stood in line with his cart piled so high he could barely see over it. He was certain that Mariel would take one look and make him haul half of it back. That was okay; he was an amateur at this profligate spending business, and mistakes were to be expected.

Mariel decided to celebrate the holiday snowfall with an early cocktail. Then she decided to go ahead and make up a pitcher. She mixed too much brandy and not enough egg nog in the blender and carried a frothing cup to the front window to watch as the yards up and down the street took on frostings of white. From upstairs, she heard music and the voices of the kids chattering back and forth. The snow, the party down the street, and the gifts stacked high and wide under the glittering tree had them excited and getting along for once.

Lucky them; this was as it should be. She hoped they'd remember, just as she recalled those rare holidays when a snowfall had arrived right on time. The memory would be something precious to cling to through the years. Something precious amidst the regrets.

She caught herself and laughed quietly at the melodrama playing in her head. *Listen to me.* Her children were healthy and they had a roof over their heads and food on the table. She had a job that wouldn't be going away. There was money in the bank; never enough but… enough. Her husband, though an incurable dreamer, was a decent man and a good father. All this was true.

She flattened her palm on a windowpane and felt the chill through the glass. A moment passed and she found herself studying the lines on the back of her hand. Though her skin was still smooth, tiny cracks and the odd tan splotch had begun to appear. Or maybe it was just her imagination. Forty-four wasn't old anymore; it was barely middle-aged. She worried too much. Somebody had to.

She pushed that thought away along with the others, took another good swallow of her drink, and allowed the brandy to mellow her mood. The panorama outside the window was as gorgeous as a postcard and she decided to stand there and enjoy it for a while.

Joe drove through the flurries with the boxes stuffing the trunk and back seat of his ancient Saab. The assault on the mall had been a gas, but he hoped the best gift of all would be waiting a few blocks away. He felt a quiver in his chest when he turned onto Church Street and pulled to the curb in front of a store that bore the weathered sign: "Brosman's Antiques."

The store occupied the middle of a forlorn trio of shops that had been pulled apart at the seams, the spaces on either side having gone long vacant. Once the mammoth retail centers had muscled in, most of Eastborough's mom-and-pop establishments had been pushed off the map. Somehow Brosman's had hung on, an old fighter sticking it out for one more round. The humble landmark had been in the same spot since Joe's childhood.

With the wipers sweeping a slow rhythm and idle music playing on the radio, he regarded the tarnished façade and recalled another snowy evening twelve years before.

It was their first Christmas as husband and wife and they had come upon Brosman's in the midst of a wonderland of clear stars and drifting white. Fresh from drinks at the pub down the street, they stopped, dazzled by the window display of an antique train hauling a cargo of jewelry through a miniature Alpine landscape, hills and vales and a tiny Swiss village, all dusted with soap-powder snow. Dark felt had been added for a night sky and a constellation of tawdry gems glittered in its folds. Entranced, Mariel tugged his arm and they stepped inside.

Even then, the place was an old photograph, amber-lit, cluttered, a little dusty, and smelling faintly of time. Mr. Brosman, the proprietor, made his slow way from his office in back to greet them. At seventy, he was short, balding, bespectacled, and dapper in shirt and tie.

Joe lingered over a selection of first edition books

near the front door while Mariel made her gradual way to a case at the back that was framed in old brass, the glass stained to a sepia tint. On one of the shelves, encased in a tiny box of thin zebrawood, was a piece that caught her eye. A little sigh came from her throat and she said, "Oh, my!"

Hearing the odd note in her voice, Joe left the books to join her.

Brosman smiled at the young couple. "Something you'd like to see?"

Mariel pointed. "What is that?"

"Ah…" The old shopkeeper slid the door open with care and produced the little box. "This…" he said, drawing out the drama, "…is called an Epiphany Star."

The pendant was an oval of amber in a setting of old gold. A ruby so blood-red that it hankered for black was the center of a four-pointed star, each ray created from a different gemstone and each producing a special gleam: a dark Czech opal, a piece of antique jade, a deep blue sapphire, and a butter-colored amethyst. More gold filigree tied the elements to one another. Even in the dark of the store, the pendant glowed as if backlit by a flickering candle.

"How old is it?" Mariel said.

"I don't know exactly," Brosman said. "A hundred years. Probably more. I know I've never seen another one like it."

Mariel said, "I think I have."

"Oh?" the old man said.

"I remember when I was a little girl my grandmother had one just like that. She never wore it. But at Christmas time, she would —"

"Drape it on a cross?" Mr. Brosman was smiling.

Mariel said, "That's right. I remember how I loved to look at it. The way it caught the light. She said she would give it to me when I grew up. But then she died and I never saw it again. I don't know what happened to it. No one knew."

"Was her family from Armenia?" Mr. Brosman inquired. When Mariel nodded, he said, "That's where this one came from."

Mariel said, "So beautiful."

"Would you like to try it on?"

She accepted the piece and let Joe hook the clasp for her, the thin gold thread all but lost in his fingers. The pendant rested at the level of her heart.

Mr. Brosman sighed and said, "Lovely. But not cheap, I'm afraid."

Joe tugged at his scarf. "How not cheap?" He

wondered if either of them heard the catch in his voice.

"The price is eight hundred dollars."

The words "Eight hundred!" were out of Joe's mouth before he could catch them.

Mariel had been gazing into the oval mirror that was perched atop the case and cupping the pendant as if it was warming her hand. Now she turned to regard Mr. Brosman soberly, her dreamy smile dipping. She said, "Oh."

"With the age of the piece and that workmanship…" Mr. Brosman was apologetic. "Any store in the city would probably charge twice that."

Joe didn't doubt it. Even so, with only one hopeful book of fiction in his agent's hands, it was far too much for their budget. The moment dragged and then seemed to stop.

He had never forgotten the look on Mariel's face as she unclasped the chain and handed back the pendant. She glanced his way and he caught a tiny blade of something in her eyes, as if it was just dawning on her what being married to the likes of Joe Kelly might mean.

For a long time after, he told himself that if he ever hit the jackpot, he'd go back and buy the piece for her. And if it was gone, he'd search the world for another, a gesture so rare that she could never be mad at him again. Whenever this came to mind, he wondered if one antique charm could make up for all the disappointments. Maybe not, but it would be a one hell of a down payment. He had imagined over and over again the surprise in her eyes when he opened the zebrawood box.

Now, after the years of driving past the store, sometimes looking, sometimes not, that particular fantasy was about to come true. He closed his eyes, opened them again. Yes, it was still Christmas Eve, snow was falling, and he was parked in front of Brosman's Antiques with money in his pocket.

He got out of the car and plodded through the new snow. The sky had shifted to an early evening indigo, the dusky half moon almost lost in clouds of dark silver.

Joe was dismayed to find the window barren. There was no sign of any little train shuttling over a magical miniature landscape and his gut sank as he leaned to the glass. Two dim lamps glowed in the back of the store and he could hear the faintest strains of music. He tried the door and to his relief, found it unlocked. A tiny bell tinkled as he pushed it open.

It wasn't the same inside, either. The shelves were almost bare and the display cases held a paltry selection of what appeared even to Joe's untrained eye to be tawdry wares. The carpet on the floor was stained and boxes stacked in the corners suggested a move in progress.

He stood in the dim quiet for a moment before calling, "Hello?"

A chair squeaked, slippers shuffled, and the Mr. Brosman Joe remembered, plus a dozen years, appeared from the office.

"Yes, sir?" The old man stared for a long few seconds. Then his eyes lit up behind thick lenses and he clasped his craggy hands together. "The Epiphany Star."

Nicole made a special effort to keep Malikah quiet as they trimmed the scrawny pine that Terry had dragged in from who knew where. It was a pathetic thing and she assumed it was a throwaway that he had snatched off the curb at one of the lots. But it was a *tree*. He hoisted it through the front door and then climbed the stairs to the attic to rummage for a half-dozen strings of lights that were coated with dust but still worked. On his second trip, he located two boxes of ornaments. He told her that all their Christmas things all been stashed away after his dad took off and hadn't been brought out since. He seemed quite pleased with himself and went off to his appointment with his rehab counselor in a flush of pride.

In the back of Nicole's mind rested a vague hope that his mom would be too hung-over or too lazy to crawl out of bed and that their Christmas would pass without an incident.

She put Malikah to work right away so that they wouldn't annoy Myra while she watched her shows. The timing worked out. Malikah was placing the last ornaments when they heard the familiar noises from the bedroom above their heads. First came muttered grunts, like a bear waking from hibernation or the devil rising for another day in hell. Footsteps shuffled along the hall to the bathroom. The toilet flushed and at the sound Nicole again dreamed of Myra falling in and then washing down the pipes, gone forever.

Next came feet clumping on the stairs and Myra appeared on the landing in her usual bathrobe and slippers. Her face was as pale as paper and stitched with wrinkles beneath a straggly mess of hair that was dyed an angry ochre. A smoking Newport jagged at a right angle from her thin lips. She stopped in the living room archway and stared at the tree. Malikah clung to her mother's side.

"Where the hell'd that come from?" Myra croaked.

"Terry found it," Nicole said.

"You mean stole it."

"Malikah did the decorations," Nicole said.

"She did, huh?" The turtle eyes slid the child's way. Malikah dipped her head shyly.

The old bitch couldn't totally resist Malikah's natural sweetness, but she had no time for Nicole, blaming her for Terry's problems, when he was the one who couldn't summon the backbone to stay clean without her propping him up. Nicole knew that if not for his mother, he'd be a different kind of man, the funny, bright, good-hearted one who surfaced enough to keep her hanging on. The same one who made promises from the bottom of his heart, like that he would steer clear of his old running partners and not even think about scoring. That he would make the meetings with his counselor without fail. That he'd talk to Myra about not being so rude. That this Christmas would be great.

So far, so good on that last one. They had pooled their resources and collected a small stack of gifts to arrange under the tree. Terry said it was the first real holiday they'd had since he was sixteen, and a sign of better times to come.

Myra broke into this daydream with a cough that sounded like a dull blade on rusty metal. She settled into her recliner with a bone-creaking groan. An inch of whiskey from the night remained in a dirty glass on the side table. Stale as it was, she'd get to it soon enough.

Her hand went scrabbling for the remote and the TV blared. This was Nicole's signal to evaporate and she shooed Malikah through the dining room and into the kitchen, leaving the old woman to her talk show. Once they were safe, Malikah rounded the kitchen table to the window and stood looking at the falling snow.

Nicole said, "That's pretty, isn't it?"

The child was quiet for a few seconds. Then she glanced over her shoulder and said, "It gonna be all right, mama?"

"Don't worry, it's going to be fine," Nicole said. She waited for Malikah to turn back to the window to let her smile fade.

Mariel had another drink, though she filled the cup only halfway, a prudent choice. She had much to do.

THE NIGHT BEFORE

She called up to the kids to finish dressing, then went about preparing an antipasto the way Joe's Italian mother had instructed her. It never failed if you lined up the right ingredients — the imported deli meats and cheeses, olives, artichokes, and so on — and then laid them down in a precise order. With a sprinkle of balsamic vinegar and olive oil as a last touch, the dish was always a hit at their parties.

Once she finished and covered the platter with plastic wrap, she moved on to the gifts. The two for Joe first, before he got back from wherever he had wandered. She had no idea. He had been acting extra odd over the last two weeks, secretive and silly, like a kid hiding something. Not that she paid that much attention to him. Or he to her, for that matter. These days, they spent a lot of time passing each other by.

Joe walked back to the car in a state of full marvel. First at the old man's memory; Brosman had drawn from a dusty corner of his mind the recollection of the couple who had wandered in from a snowy evening long ago and how the pretty woman had been mesmerized by the Epiphany Star. Then, like a wizard performing a special magic, he puttered and muttered for an absent minute before producing the zebrawood box from the secret place it had rested for all that time. He opened it with fingers that trembled with age.

The pendant was as Joe remembered it, untarnished by the years. "I can't believe it's still here," he murmured.

"Maybe it's been waiting for you," the old man said. "I guess it's your lucky night."

The price on the item was the same and to their mutual delight, Joe counted the eight hundred-dollar bills into the storekeeper's palm. Except for the surprise part, he wished Mariel had been there to see. Mr. Brosman walked him to the door and they spent a moment looking out at the snow.

"Reminds me of when I was a boy," the old man said. "Every Christmas should be like this. But then it wouldn't be so special, would it?" He patted Joe's shoulder, wished him a happy holiday, and then locked the door behind him. By the time Joe got into his car and started the wipers, the lights in the store had gone off, as if it hadn't been open at all. In a moment of panic, he went digging into his coat pocket. The zebrawood box felt warm to his touch.

―

The kids tried to dash out the door, but Mariel snapped them back and made them stand for inspection. She didn't have to worry about Christian. He had spent his upstairs time finding something nice to wear, then combing his hair and brushing his teeth. Hannah was the one who required checking. She was her father's daughter and would leave the house wearing a patchwork of whatever she first laid hands on or struck her odd fancy. Sometimes the ensemble worked and sometimes she looked like a child's bad drawing.

Tonight she had chosen well and came up with something like a Dickens character, with a blouse, vest, pedal-pushers, knee socks, saddle shoes, and a cute hat.

They were jumping up and down, eager to leave. Betsy had come up with the idea of starting the kids' party early and letting them burn off their energies and wind down to TV and games in the basement in time for the parents to arrive for the grown-up fun.

Mariel let them bolt, then watched as they skittered down the walk and into the street, the snow now packed by passing cars. They left an echoing silence in their wake and she stood still for a while, lost in her thoughts.

During the drive home, Joe mulled strategies for presenting the Epiphany Star and the news of the book deal. He settled on laying a sweet trap. Instead of just handing her the gift, he'd leave it with the copy of the check and the crumpled slip from the ATM and then hide to watch as she made the discovery.

Like a thief casing a joint, he plotted the house in his head and settled on the kitchen table. He could wait in the darkness of the dining room for the delicious instant when she realized that her loser of a husband had just knocked one out of the park. If he staged it correctly, her face would be cast in the light of the hanging lamp, an image he'd hold in his mind forever.

Would she believe her eyes when she happened upon the zebrawood box? Would she even remember that long-ago visit to Brosman's?

Of course she would; Mariel forgot nothing. Over the years, she had counted his failures like beads, recording every one of them, though to her credit this was not out of spite. He knew the mental list was a shield against expecting too much and having her discontent sour into resentment.

Even so, in his most honest moments, he guessed if

it wasn't for his parenting, she would have set him adrift years ago. She valued that. It was also true that she had once admired his refusal to give up on his books, never lording it over him that she was the primary breadwinner. Those sands had shifted over time, too. With the sales of the first novel dead (how that was about to change!) and the other two unable to earn back even their modest advances in spite of great reviews, her respect for his craft had worn thin.

Now and then, he caught her watching him work with her brow stitched with petulant lines, as if broadcasting her impatience with his silliness. When he proffered some word of blind hope about one of the books, she would respond with a roll of her eyes and a sigh, just as she did when she was exasperated with one of the kids.

Joe decided he would accept her apology, verbal or unspoken, graciously.

Hannah and Christian would hear the incredible news come morning, to go with the presents their parents would wrap during the wee hours as they polished off the pricey bottle of pinot. The thought reminded him of the first night that they had slept together and he wondered if his good luck meant some of that magic would be revived, too.

Turning on to his street, he saw sliding, tumbling, snow-crusted children in front of every house and slowed to a crawl. The looks on their ruddy faces and their joyous laughter as they went careening through the clouds of fluttering white brought a small throb in his chest. Brosman was right: this was how Christmas was supposed to be. Given the state of the climate, it might not happen again while these kids were young.

His next-door neighbor Don was in his driveway, fiddling with his snow blower. God forbid a few flakes marred the beauty of his newly-resealed macadam. He straightened as Joe pulled into the garage, offering a wave and his customary frown. Don owned two vehicles, a Lexus and some SUV thing the size of a tour bus, and was perpetually offended by Joe's rundown import.

Well, fuck you and your gas hogs. Old Don was in for a surprise, too. Not that Joe had ever cared what he thought.

He found Mariel dashing about in dizzy circles, her cell phone on and off her ear as she hurried from room to room, getting ready for their Christmas Eve and morning. Her greeting was a small, blank smile cast in his general direction. He took a bottle of water from the fridge and watched for her a few moments.

She was still a handsome woman, though in the last couple years she had gone a little hard around the edges in both her looks and her temperament. They had been an odd match, something like the princess and the stable boy; and yet he could fairly say that he still loved her, and guessed that they spent more time engaged in carnal acts than most couples who had been married as long.

She ended her call and looked his way. "So?"

Joe stifled the grin that was lurking behind his eyes and came up with a vague shrug. "I got most of the things on the list," he said. "But I'm going back out. A couple more stores and then I'll go grab a drink with Billy."

"Of course. What's Christmas without boozing with Billy?"

It came out a little snide, but Joe was in too good a mood to let it bother him and just laughed. Mariel responded with a smile that was not unkind.

"So I can expect you when?"

"I don't know. Eight, maybe. Not before."

"I've got an errand to run, but I'll be back by then," she said. "I made the antipasto, so we can just go." She was turning away when he touched her shoulder and planted a quiet kiss on her mouth. "Well," she said, blinking. The sudden affection had caught her off guard.

"It's Christmas Eve," he said.

He did catch up with Billy. That much of what he told Mariel was true. Her claim that no holiday was the same without his old friend's barroom cheer was also true. Though she did not mean it as a compliment.

Billy Alden was the type girls adored when they were young, single, and wild, and dismissed or despised forever after. He was a first-class maniac and true gypsy, and so he remained the kind of magnetic force who could tempt even the most stalwart husband into delinquency. More than a few of the women in their social circle had waited out his clownish impositions, steaming in private until the rings were on their fingers so they could say, "All right, get rid of him."

Some of the husbands did just that. Joe stood firm. He had known Billy since grade school and loved him like an errant brother. For her part, Mariel had resigned herself to his presence, though she hadn't allowed him around the house since the night he made a drunken pass at her mother. She told Joe she found it ridiculous that a man well into middle age went by "Billy." What was he, seven? A circus midget? That was as far as her nagging went. The man was like an old car that got towed from one garage to the next, never running quite right, an eyesore but a harmless hobby.

Joe found the eyesore hunkered down in a booth at the Delaware Tavern, his home away from home. Melinda, the pretty red-haired waitress that Billy lusted after, came out from behind the bar.

"Joe," she said. "Merry Christmas."

"I'll have a gimlet," Joe said. "And make it with Grey Goose." Melinda murmured her surprise. Joe glanced Billy's way. "And my friend will have?"

Billy raised an eyebrow. "You still got that bottle of single-malt? Lag... Laga..."

"Lagavulin?" Melinda said. "That's forty-five dollars a pour."

Joe flicked one of his hundreds onto her tray. "And have something for yourself," he said.

The barmaid stared at the crisp bill. "You win the lottery?"

"Let's just say it's my lucky night." Joe slid into the

booth. He allowed a moment of silent drama before producing the zebrawood box, a sleight-of-hand artist presenting a dove from a hat.

Billy studied the pendant and said, "I really wanted the '67 Telecaster from that vintage store in Philly. But thanks. I love you, too." His red face opened into the impish grin that women had once found irresistible. "Is that it, man? Really?"

"Still there, after twelve years. And that ain't all." He laid a copy of the check alongside it.

"That's his signature?" Billy said.

"His manager's," Joe explained. "These guys don't sign the checks. But it's the real deal. The money's in the bank." He spent another few dumbstruck seconds mulling the proof of what had transpired in the last weeks. Sensing the weight of the moment, Billy refrained from grabbing the pendant in one of his paws or making a crude joke. A muted flash of envy for Joe's happy ending crossed his green eyes and then went away, replaced by deep kindness.

"Merry Christmas. You deserve it, bro." He shook his head over the pendant nestled in the little box and the copy of the check and said, "Man, she is going to fuck you blind."

THE NIGHT BEFORE

Once the kids were gone and the presents wrapped and arranged under the tree, Mariel treated herself to another drink. The Junghaus on the dining room wall chimed twice for the half-hour. She studied the face of the clock, musing about all the time it had marked since they received it as a wedding present from Joe's father, who had brought it back from Germany.

Her thoughts drifted on and she had to stop and remind herself why she'd been looking at the damn thing in the first place. She returned to the front window and within a few minutes, saw two bundled figures on the driveway next door: Caroline and her daughter Kimberly heading for the party. Of course, Caroline was going early to help Betsy. It was the kind of thing she did, the perpetual volunteer. Mariel sipped her drink and gazed out on the street. She had just drained the last drops when she heard a knock at the back door.

After another half-hour, another gimlet, and a crazy-ass argument about how best to spend his "movie money," Joe left Billy lying in wait for some lonely woman looking to collect a stray to warm her bed on this special night.

Outside, the sky had darkened to a wine purple that

was dappled with faint early stars. Joe laid his gloves on the dashboard and listened to an a capella choir chanting Bach as he waited for the engine to warm. He experienced another few seconds of minor alarm when he couldn't find the zebrawood box amidst the folds of his coat. Then he located it, tucked snugly in an inside pocket.

He drove out of the lot to find that the busy activity on the streets had slowed to a trickle, leaving only stragglers. He stopped at the State Store for a bottle and drove the rest of the way home reviewing the choreography of what was to be a miraculous evening. The dance began with him drifting to the curb on Birch Lane, one street over from their house. Pulling up the hood of his jacket, he hopped out and cut between the houses and across the yards to the rear door of the garage, the one they rarely used.

He had unlocked it earlier and now the latch slid back with the tiniest click. He pushed it open just wide enough to sidle through and closed it behind him, muffling the sound with the weight of his body. He took a step, bumped directly into the fender of Mariel's Beemer, and stood in the darkness, confused. Hadn't she said she was going out somewhere? He couldn't remember anything about catching a ride with one of her friends, but it was not unlikely. Or maybe her plans had changed. If she was in the house, he'd have to arrange for the surprise later.

Creeping around the sedan, he stepped into the laundry room and closed the door behind him. From somewhere in the house, he heard a voice down low and guessed that Mariel or one of the kids had left a radio on. When he moved into the pantry, he caught an odd scrabbling sound, and wondered if their dog Peanut had gotten into something. With the zebrawood box clutched tight in one hand and the copy of the check and the ATM slip in the other, he inched his way into the kitchen. The urgent sounds were now louder and he guessed they were coming from the TV; except there was no blue light from the main room. He crept across the kitchen to the dining room archway and stopped.

Mariel was bent over the table with her dress hiked above her waist. The buttons of her blouse were undone and one strap of her brassiere hung loose to the side. Her head was bent down and her eyes drawn tight as if she was in the throes of a ferocious prayer and she moaned a kind of slow music.

Don, the one with the riding mower and snow blower, gripped her shoulders as he shoved his pelvis against her in a slow grind, his eyes closed tighter than hers. Their movements were as one, and among the jumble that came roaring through Joe's brain was the thought that this wasn't the first time they'd done this.

Though he hadn't moved or made a sound, Mariel sensed his presence, because she pulled out of her swoon in a sudden second and gasped, "Don? Don!" She cast her eyes about and saw Joe, or at least his shape, a specter looming in the darkness, and the groan that came from her throat tore her last gasp of passion neatly in half.

In the next second, Don saw him, too, yelped out a curse, jumped back, and launched into a clumsy jig, grabbing his trousers to keep them from falling with one hand while flapping the other in the air as if to wave Joe into invisibility. Mariel's arms trembled as she pushed her skirt down and clutched her blouse. Her mouth was a jagged slash and fear and tears were springing from her eyes.

Joe stood petrified in sick fascination as he watched this slapstick. His mind went blank, even as he felt his heart crack into fragments and sink through his chest. He staggered under the rage that rose up in a black wave, but in the next moment, it was gone, sucked out of him, and he turned away and made a stumbling retreat, through the kitchen and garage and into the December night, leaving a vacuum of shock in his wake.

The snow was coming down in random swirls, riding the cold wind. What had fallen during the day was packed and Joe slipped and stumbled in a crazy zigzag through the Hamblins' yard.

His breath shot out before him as if he had eaten fire, his heart felt like a clenched fist, his teeth chattered, and his vision had gone blurry. Reeling into a swing set, he was treated to a surreal slide show: Mariel folded over with her blouse hanging open; her horrified face and Don's gape of fear; the pendulum of the wall clock tick-tocking solemn time above the three characters posing in rigid alarm.

Just as he reached the street, tires crunched on ice and he stopped and swung around with his jaw set for Mariel and fists clenched in case it was Don. No matter that he had lost every fight in his life except one twenty years before. He was ready to slug it out. But the car, a Saturn wagon, rolled by and neither one of the villains appeared out of the drifting flakes, mobile or on foot.

He slowed his steps and the wall collapsed. Another set of images of the two of them fastened together, back to front, brought a churn in his gut that tasted of bile, and then a spike in his heart so sharp that it buckled his knees. For a few seconds, he verged on going down in a crumpled mess to melt the fallen snow with his own hot tears. His next thought was of the kids. He saw before him their faces alight with the delights of the season and wanted to cry. At that instant, they were having a terrific time at Betsy's party, unaware that their parents' marriage had just tumbled into a sinkhole.

The moment of crushing heartache passed. He caught his breath and plodded back to his car. The zebrawood box jumped to mind, eight hundred bucks in gems and gold, and he performed a frantic mime, slapping his pockets with his right hand until he realized that the box was still clasped in his left, so tightly that one corner had torn a hole in the palm of his glove.

This relief was caught short when he couldn't find his car keys and realized that he had dropped them somewhere, inside the house or outside in the snow. Either way, there was no going back for them. So he walked on.

The windows of the houses that he passed were cast in shades of cheery white, gold, and green, with multicolored coronas of lights and the Jolly St. Nicks and nativities arrayed before frosted panes of glass that framed glittering trees. Parties were in full holiday tilt at several of the houses, and he wondered blankly what betrayals were taking place inside those warm walls.

The two of them had done it before. He knew this to be true. He had witnessed their ease, old hands who knew each other's fleshly contours. For how long had it been going on? Months? Years? Since she decided that her husband was never going to be a true provider, meaning a real man like Don?

Yes, Don was that sort, the kind of breadwinner who owned a 54-inch television set, hired people to landscape his lawn, and treated the family to Mexico Beach for not one but two weeks every summer. Every year, they invited Joe and Mariel to bring the kids down for a weekend, but it had never worked out. Joe suspected that Don was most interested in seeing Mariel in a bikini. An unfounded suspicion, as it turned out. He laughed sourly into the silent night. Don wouldn't care about a glimpse of Mariel's bare flesh. He'd seen all he wanted in their dining room and who knew what other parts of the house?

Joe wondered if Don's wife Caroline had any inkling. Maybe it would be his pleasure to tell her.

Breathless with exertion and heartache, he stopped and looked around. He had reached High Street. If he kept on, he'd be hiking over Hanover Street and arrive on the banks of the river. The last thing he needed was to be alone with his thoughts, swinging in a wild arc between despair and murderous anger, a blue swirl of sorrow followed by dreams of homicide. So he stomped in a circle, yelling curses into the starlit night, in such a state that he didn't notice the pickup until the lights were on him. The truck pulled to a stop and the window rolled down.

"You okay?" The driver's red face was too jolly.

Joe said, "Yeah, okay," and waved him away.

"All right, then. Merry Christmas." The window slid up and the truck started forward.

"Merry fuck you," Joe snarled.

The truck stopped and the window rolled down once more. The driver poked his head out. The jolly had disappeared. "What'd you say?"

"What did *you* say?" Joe was barking at the moon.

"I said 'Merry Christmas.'"

Joe shook his head as if trying to loose it from his

neck. "Yeah, whatever…"

The driver said, "You need to go home, my friend." The truck started off again.

"Hey, wait a minute!" Joe hollered.

Mariel tottered from one room to the next and then climbed the staircase with Don edging along behind, his face blanched except for a red patch on each cheek and the bead of sweat above his lip.

"Oh, my God!" she wailed. "I don't believe this. Jesus Christ!"

Don wore the look of a man who wanted to run for his life; because he was afraid of Caroline finding out, of what Joe might do, or both. Mariel knew her husband wasn't the type to pick fights; even so, he had a temper. That he had never raised a hand to the kids didn't mean he was a wimp. He stayed in shape and she could imagine him tearing into Don. They had never liked each other. As to Caroline, she would take whatever her husband dished out. More than once, Don had whispered in Mariel's ear what a lousy lay his wife was, another feature of her jellyfish nature.

She reeled into the bathroom, feeling her stomach heave. When Don tried to follow, she slammed the door in his face, then locked it. She put a hand on the edge of the sink to steady herself and closed her eyes tight. What had she been thinking? The next-door neighbor? What was she, trailer trash? The town slut who couldn't keep her panties up for five minutes? What if one of the kids had surprised them?

Her heart hammered as she imagined the crack in her world turning into spider web of fractures and then breaking into a tumble of shards. There was no way to fix what had happened. She couldn't trust Don to keep his mouth shut. He might even run home and confess to Caroline. Yes, that would be him, all right. He'd get a jump, blame it all on the jezebel next door, and present it as a chance for husband and wife to reaffirm their bonds of marriage.

Of course Caroline would swallow whatever bullshit he spouted. After which she'd spread the word around the neighborhood. The phones and internet connections would be humming. Someone would find out at the office and Mariel Kelly would be gossip headline number one. And for what? A few sweaty couplings driven by a desperate urge that amounted to her midlife crisis. And just to make sure she couldn't construct any worse of a disaster, it had come to a crashing climax the night before Christmas.

The disgust convulsed her stomach and she leaned over the toilet to let its sour contents come up in a noisy, stinging rush. When she finished, she rose shakily, washed out her mouth, and brushed her teeth. Then she opened the small window to let the cold air calm her rioting brain, if only for a few seconds.

She had no choice but to put up a front and hope for the best. Which meant she would have to get dressed and go to the party. Don would show up, too and Caroline and the rest of their neighbors would be there to greet her. She'd make an excuse for Joe's absence and maintain a game face, smiling and chatting even as she was crumbling inside. What else could she do?

Her heartbeat slowed and she spent a moment gazing out over the snow-crusted rooftops, wondering where her husband had gone and trying to imagine what would happen when he came home.

The Reverend Franklin Callum of The Light of the World Tabernacle stood watching the snow settle on the windowsill. Tall and round in the middle, his cheeks were fringed in a white beard. His eyes were dark and intense, but mostly benign. Only the closest inspection would discover blades of despair hidden in their depths.

The reverend was musing on the blessed weather when his assistant Willie stepped into the office. He offered a smile as Willie handed him the keys to the van. "How are the streets out there?"

"They getting slick," Willie said. "But it was all right."

"You need to get on," Reverend Callum said.

"I can stay," Willie said. "I don't mind."

The reverend waved him out with a gentle hand. "No, your family will be waiting."

The two men walked through the tiny chapel to the front door. The reverend turned the key in the lock and they stood watching the silver flakes falling from the night sky.

Willie said, "You know you're welcome to come spend the evening with us."

The reverend shook his head. "Someone might need me. Imagine being out on a night like this with no place to go?" He saw the look on Willie's gentle face and said, "Don't you worry. I'll be fine right here."

Willie stepped outside. "Well, then, the blessings of the night and the day on you, Reverend."

"And the same to you and your family," the

reverend offered. He watched Willie tramp off down the sidewalk, then closed and locked the door. He had just settled back into his office with a cup of coffee when the phone rang.

The truck rolled south on Third Street and by the time they reached the river, the driver had clearly had enough of his passenger's grim silence and was too happy to dump him. They mumbled at each other as Joe stepped to the curb.

Though downtown glowed in an inviting way, Joe instead crossed the bridge, gazing now and then into the icy black water. The night and the streets were quieter and houses smaller on the other side, the Christmas lights hanging in haphazard strings as if advertising the disorder of the lives inside or absent altogether. The snow had receded to a gentle flutter.

Huffing along in no particular direction, he shoved his thoughts off his misery and instead buried them in practical matters. He didn't know what he would do now. How could he face Mariel? How could she face him? How could he enter their dining room and not see her and Don clawing at each other? And what of the kids? What would the backwash of this sad and crazy mess do to them?

He stopped walking, stilled by the revelation that his life would never be the same again. He might not be able to go back at all.

At the next corner, he dug out his cell and saw that he had no messages. This was not a surprise. Mariel would be in the throes of shock at getting caught. He thought about calling Billy, but his friend left his phone off most of the time, claiming one day that the devices caused brain cancer and the next that they were an insidious way for the government to spy on truant citizens like him. Joe knew he could try the Delaware, but in truth, he wasn't ready to share the bad news. The shame would be too much. He could hear his friend's voice rough voice: *That bitch! Are you kidding me? On the table? What a whore!*

He stopped at a quiet intersection. A few flakes circled helplessly to the cold ground, as lost as he was. He heard the weary sound of a car on the next street over spinning tires.

Peering down the block, he caught sight of a sign flashing red and green against the white landscape. In an instant of dull surprise, he realized that his errant shoes had carried him back to the edge of his old neighborhood. The sign beckoned and he started walking.

Jimmy's was a memory that went back to when he was a squirt. His father had taken him there on Friday nights when he wanted to give his wife a break.

The bar had been a mysterious place to a small boy, a cavern of muted light, shadows, and whispers. Joe remembered how they would arrive to a small fanfare. His dad would lead him to the bar and sit him on the end stool. The bartender would present a cherry Coke as if he was serving a duke. The regulars, many of them lone drunkards, doted on him. When he got to be a little older, he saw the cracks behind the smiles and in the pained, bleary eyes. There was never any music, only hard laughter lifted on the smoky breaths of workingmen. A woman with a painted face would sometimes make a drunken fuss over him until the bartender chased her away. No one wanted her likes around a child, and Joe could still see the stark expression of pain on her face when they ran her off, as if she'd been struck and wanted to weep.

Later, Jimmy's was one of the few joints where teenagers could buy beer any time of day or night and rumors floated about all kinds of vice inside those smoky walls.

That had all been a long time ago and it never

occurred to him that the tavern would still be standing. It had been years since he had passed this way. Now he tramped along the sidewalk to stand beneath the sign of red and green neon in a rusting metal box. With not another welcoming light in sight, he climbed the steps and pushed the door open.

The room had shrunk, with the long bar and the Formica tables with the tube metal legs that he had negotiated as a child cramped together beneath a low ceiling. The once-mellow lights were now as gaudy as swabs of cheap lipstick and the air in the room was close, laden with decades of sweat, rough tobacco, and stale liquor.

Two men perched like twin buzzards at opposite ends of the bar and a woman sat alone at the table in the far corner. The bartender was thin and ferret-faced, his ropy arms scrawled with old tattoos. The three men regarded Joe with hooded gazes as he made his way to the middle of the bar.

"Help ya?" The bartender made no move in Joe's direction, assuming that he had gotten lost or had car trouble.

Joe pulled off his gloves and perused the bottles on the shelf. "You have a decent Irish whiskey?"

It required several seconds for the bartender to

understand that the visitor was a paying customer. Then he didn't seem to care much for the idea, taking his sweet time to poke around until he located a bottle of Bushmill's, which he held up for inspection.

"That's fine," Joe said, unzipping his coat. "Double, straight up." He glanced down the bar. "A round for the others," he said. "And one for you, too."

The bartender hiked a hard eyebrow, poured Joe's whiskey, and then went about pulling draughts for the twins and mixing a Seabreeze for the lady at the table. The older of the two men grunted something that might have been a thank you.

The bartender placed the cocktail on a coaster and called, "Gina? Man bought a round for the house." He helped himself to a shot of the Bushmill's, throwing it back like a pro. Joe laid a twenty and a ten on the bar and said, "Keep it."

The bartender cocked his head as if he mistrusted Joe's intentions. After a moment's pause, he shrugged, picked up the bills, rapped his knuckles on the polished wood, and moved off to stock a cooler.

Joe planted an elbow, leaning his cheek into his palm. "I'll Be Home for Christmas" was playing softly in the background, like someone's idea of a joke. Mariel and Don appeared to him again in their lurid coupling, this time in slow motion. It had all transpired in the space of a few seconds, and yet something told him he'd hold the images in his mind for a long time. He took a fast wallop of his whiskey, settled the glass on the bar, and gazed moodily into the amber liquor, feeling a smoky heat settle in his head and gut. Minutes passed as he wandered down a dark road, drawing more pictures of bloody murder. The nausea made another visit and went away.

Something moved in the corner of his eye and he turned to see that the woman from the table had stepped to the bar to claim her drink. She was peeking at him from under a shock of hair. Her smile was uncertain. She said, "Joe?"

It had been almost thirty years and it took a few seconds to fill in the woman's face. "Gina Marinelli," he said. For that brief moment, the awful drama that had landed him there was shoved aside by the thought that he knew someone on the premises.

Or at least remembered her. She, Marie Petrucci, and Donna Amato had run together at school, a three-headed monster that had always reminded him of the Shangri-Las. They had been wild and flashy, splashed with too much makeup, their hair cut spiky and dyed various colors, dressed in thrift-store ensembles that listed to black, real Italian girls who weren't afraid of the boys.

Was it Gina who had knocked Benny Hess on his ass in back of the Sunshine Lanes or had that been one of the others? He thought to ask her, then changed his mind. That younger world was no place for a glum cuckold on the night before Christmas.

He couldn't recall the last time he had seen her. In school, they had existed in different orbits. Afterwards, he had spent years wandering gypsy roads before coming back to start his family, work at whatever he could, and put words to paper. What he had to show for it was two beautiful children, a career that had just been raised from the dead, and a marriage that was rolling in the opposite direction.

Was that the deal? A trade-off? Had a bargain with the devil been made without his knowledge? That would explain the entwined strokes of luck, one fabulous and the other terrible.

He sensed Gina watching him and pulled himself out of his tailspin to look her over. She had been adorable in a funky way back when. Now the cute had given way to middle age. Her hair was short and bottle black and the olive cast of her skin had gone pale. She was wearing jeans and a blouse that was too light for the weather. She looked tired, though running into an old classmate seemed to have buoyed her spirits, bringing little points of light to her dark eyes.

He said, "What are you doing here?"

"You know," she said. "My dad owned it since we were in school."

Joe now recalled that Mr. Marinelli had been the proprietor of various gin mills around Eastborough. There had always been something faintly suspect about the man and the talk had his hands in all sorts of murky business. Though there was nothing in doubt about the way he treated the boys, as if every one was a threat to his youngest daughter's virginity. It was a big joke, as Joe recalled, because in Gina's case, that bird had long since flown.

The princess from this ancient opera broke into his thoughts. "I read something about you in the newspaper," she said. "You wrote a book."

"Three," he told her. "Had three published, I mean."

He thought over spouting off about the option, but it seemed such a hollow victory now. Win the big prize, but lose the girl to the snake that had been lurking in the bushes all along. "That was a while ago," he finished.

"So that's what you do," she said. "Write books."

"And other things." It sounded more feeble with every word and he hoped she'd change the subject.

She did. "So, you still live in Eastborough?"

"Crescent Drive," he said. "It's up near the —"

"I know where it is." She glanced down at the ring on his finger. "And you're married."

"Yeah." He got it out quickly, adding: "Nobody you would have known."

"Kids?"

"Two. A girl and a boy." He blinked and looked away from her, feeling as if he'd taken a punch. After a fast sip of his whiskey, he said, "And what about you?"

If she heard the odd note in his voice, she gave no sign. "What about me?" she said.

"Married? Divorced? Boyfriend? Girlfriend?"

Her mouth dipped and her eyes cooled and shifted. "I was married, yeah. Do you remember Kevin Sammons?"

Joe conjured a fuzzy photo of an upperclassman.

"Lasted five years and I was out the door. No kids." Now it was she who didn't want to linger. "So what brings you in here?" she said.

Joe said, "Just out for a drink."

She produced a dim smile. "And you didn't have anywhere else to go?"

She hadn't said, "better," though that was what she meant. "Not much open," he said.

She was regarding him with her head tilted slightly back. He figured she was trying to guess the real reason why he had wandered into a seedy saloon in a dark corner of town on this of all nights.

Before she could grill him further, he said, "You know my dad use to bring me here."

Gina said, "Oh, yeah? How old were you?"

"Little," he said. "Five or six. You could do that then. Bring kids into a bar." He thought for a moment about those long ago times and then the odd arc that had brought him to that same location and to Gina Marinelli so many years later.

She took a turn and told him a little more about herself. She had gone to community college, then dropped out because the old man needed help with the bar and she was the only one of the siblings who had an interest. She had taken off and bummed around some. Mexico was nice, she said, and would have stayed on a beach forever, but her dad passed away and left Jimmy's to her. Now she mostly lived by night.

Joe understood that there was more, most of her life, in fact. But he wasn't inclined to ask about it and she didn't offer anything further. He ordered another round for the two of them, leaving the bartender and his customers to fend for themselves. The drinks arrived and they fell silent, thinking their own thoughts.

As if they'd been waiting for a cue, Joe's kids reappeared, this time in a cloudy vignette. A wave of emotion washed over him as he pictured their sweet faces. They were truly his life. And now what, now that he had discovered their mother's treachery? How would they go on? The bile rose again and he felt another bolt of sick wrath at what she had done to them.

He cracked his glass down on the bar, spilling some of the whiskey over his hand. Gina reached for some napkins. She dabbed his hand and the bar. With a glance his way, she said. "Are you all right?"

Joe lifted his glass and then put it down again.

She touched his arm. "You have trouble at home?"

Joe thought to put a game face on, but then said, "Yeah, kind of… yeah."

She gazed upon him with a frank sympathy. "And tonight, yet."

He swallowed hard. The last thing he wanted to do was break down and start bawling in front of her, the two mugs, and the tattooed bartender. The cartoon that played in his head sent him around a corner and instead he coughed up a laugh.

Gina said, "What?"

"It's nothing." He didn't want the drink and didn't want to be in that lonely dive anymore. The whole mess was so odd and sad that even his astounding news couldn't wash it clean. Any more than the thick wad of bills in his pocket could ransom his anguish.

Gina caught the vibe and said, "What is it?"

"I think I need to go home," he said.

He was standing on the sidewalk, pulling on his gloves, when he heard Gina call to him. She was framed in the doorway, her arms crossed against the chill of the night.

"You're not going home, are you?" she said.

Joe shook his head. "No. I'm not."

She watched him for a few seconds before saying, "Come back inside while I get my coat."

Nicole had whispered a silent prayer that it would be okay, that things would stay calm through the evening and into Christmas morning. So far, Myra was minding her own business, parked in the front room with the TV blaring canned laughter and her jelly glass of Seagram's on the end table. With any luck, she'd drink herself back into a nodding stupor and sleep through the night.

Peeking from the kitchen doorway, Nicole could see the corona of curlers beginning a downward tilt. It was a good sign, though by no means were they out of danger. She sensed something in the air, a bitter energy that was all too familiar. And for all her hoping, she couldn't hold back the tidal wave when it rose up to drown their Christmas Eve.

She had just given Malikah a snack and had gone back to finishing the ribbon on the last of the gifts when Terry came in the door. She heard him muttering about something and then he appeared in the kitchen doorway. The dull-eyed, dopey look on his face told her that their night was about to go wrong.

"How was your meeting?" she said.

Terry pulled his eyes off the gaily-wrapped package. "My what?"

"Your meeting," she said. "With your counselor. How did it go?"

Terry said, "It went, uh…"

Nicole knew. He hadn't made his rehab appointment at all. She was on him, pulling up his sleeve with a rough motion. When she saw the fresh tracks, she jerked his arm as if trying to pull it out of its socket.

"You scored?" her voice went up. "With what?" He gaped at her, his face a cartoon of slow wit. "With what?" She turned around and grabbed her bag from the counter.

Myra called from the front room. "Terry! Get in here, goddamnit!"

Nicole tossed the bag back on the counter and fixed a hard eye on him. "You took the money."

"Terry!"

Malikah said, "Mama…"

Now Myra was screeching. "Now!"

Terry mumbled something and backed away from Nicole. He wouldn't meet her eyes as he disappeared through the doorway.

"I had forty damn dollars here," Myra was raging. "Did you take it? Answer me. Or was it her?"

Nicole felt her face getting hot. She made a beeline for the living room. Myra was out of her chair, waving her purse in the air. "Did you take my money?"

Nicole glared back at her. "I never took a dime from you, Myra." She clenched her fists to keep herself from slapping the old bitch's face. There had never been any doubt that the woman was a racist, the small-town, white trash, bred-in-the-bone kind. She railed about the coons on the street and the jungle-bunnies on TV, even when Nicole and Malikah were in the room. Now she went into overdrive.

"I said I want her out of here, goddamnit!" Myra shrieked. "You hear me?"

Terry was sniveling. "Ma…" His eyes were red and brimming.

Myra was raging. "Out of this goddamn house!" she screeched. "Right now."

An echoing silence descended. A few seconds went by and Terry turned around again. It was if his skin had been stripped away, leaving a sick, weak skeleton in full view.

Nicole understood instantly. She turned around and kneeled down. "Go get your coat on," she whispered. Malikah started to sniffle. "Don't cry, baby."

She bundled her daughter while Myra muttered curses and Terry shook and moaned. Keeping her back to Malikah, Nicole glared at him. "You sonofabitch," she said. "It's Christmas." If she could have gotten her hands on the pistol he kept stashed upstairs, she might have shot the both of them.

Malikah was whimpering as they fled into the raw night. Nicole fixed Myra with a last look that froze the woman's tongue, even as her son sobbed in the background. Malikah held out her hands for the gaily-wrapped presents and wailed.

Neither the bartender nor either of the two lonely customers looked up when they went out the door again. The night had turned crystalline and the snow had dampened the cold. They tramped unsteadily down Ferry Street. Gina's coat was threadbare, a funky piece from a thrift store rack. She told Joe not to worry; she was warm enough.

He hoped she wasn't following him because he didn't know where he was going. After every few steps he thought about wishing her good night and turning for home. He wondered if the kids had missed him yet. Probably not; it was still early and they had the party at Betsy's. Then he wondered if Mariel was taking comfort from Don, who had to be in a panic of his own. Would they show their faces at the party? They'd have to. Joe took a moment's comfort at imagining Don's fake jovial laugh and Mariel's blanching face, both of them wondering if any second he'd come bursting through the door, ready to ruin both their lives.

Gina now trudged ahead of him through the soft snow, talking over her shoulder as she passed on high school history in breathless snippets. "You hear about Ray Fegler? He shot his ex-wife." Then, "Carmine Zitelli. He played football, you remember? He got AIDs and died." And, "Hey, whatever happened to Billy Alden, that guy you used to hang with?" Only after she stopped walking did he hear her last question. "So, you want to come up?"

She had stopped at a doorway lodged between two storefronts where Fourth and Queen streets crossed. Joe said, "This is…"

"My place," she said. "Where I live."

The furnishings weren't much, all worn and stuffed into two small rooms. The walls were a dingy off-white and the string of lights over the street windows sagged into something like a clown's sad smile. This was where her life had placed her after the almost thirty years since they'd left school.

She produced a bottle of wine from a kitchen cabinet and poured two glasses. Joe sipped, found it sweet and not to his liking. She dug out a pack of Marlboros and lit up without offering him one.

She wouldn't meet his eyes. He understood; in the space of an hour, they had gone from forgetting that the other one existed to the intimacy of a dark, quiet abode. He was absently aware that the door to the dark bedroom was half-open and let himself consider that there was seduction in progress. She was not a young girl, flaunting her freedom. She was in her forties, alone and lonely, and craving. She seemed to read these thoughts, knew he knew her secret, and was ashamed.

"Sorry about the wine," she said and tried for a laugh that didn't work. The tip of her cigarette glowed from a shadow.

Joe crossed the room to stand at the window. Using the side of his fist to clear the frost, he looked out to see that the snow had stopped falling on the white-quilted streets and sidewalks.

With his back to Gina and the cramped room and gazing out at this winter wonderland, it occurred to him that he had known all along in some corner of his gut that Mariel had betrayed him. Not just once, and maybe not just with Don, either. He guessed that she had told herself that the dalliances were her right and

THE NIGHT BEFORE

his punishment, payback for his failures. Going back to that long ago evening in Brosman's and the Epiphany Star.

As the years passed, he had not been so blind as to miss the light in her eyes shifting away from him. What had happened to the dreams — no, the promises — of fame and riches? They had been dumped at the side of the road, the reality of the work he had chosen. So why, when it dawned on her that he was such a loser, didn't she pack up the kids and leave or tell him to hit the road, Jack? Same story; because she would not cheat the children out of a decent father. She was not a bad woman and in that respect, had done the right thing.

At the same time, he had been unwilling to face the forlorn drama that was coming his way like a rumbling train. So Don wasn't the first. Other men had taken his wife, spread her legs, mounted her from front and back, and she had in turn done all sorts of delicious erotic things to them. Meanwhile, he raised their son and daughter and tried to make something magical appear on sheets of 80-pound paper.

Out of the shadows, Gina said, "What was that?" and he realized he had muttered something.

"She said she'd give me a year to finish the book,

another year to sell it. And then find a real job."

Gina shifted her position on the couch and said, "Oh?"

"But, I didn't. Find the job, I mean."

That had been their agreement, his and Mariel's. He managed to bring in a little money with the first book, next to nothing from the other two. He floundered about with freelance work and teaching and his wife came to understand that she had married a noble fool.

Gina said, "So what's her name?"

Joe hesitated, feeling that he was starting down a crooked path. How much did he want this stranger to know?

"It's Mariel," he said at last.

"And the kids?"

"Hannah and Christian," he said and swallowed.

"What about the other guy?"

He turned around and settled on the windowsill, feeling the chilled glass through the back of his sweater. He couldn't make out Gina's face or read the tone of her voice. He spent a moment wondering if he had given some clue or if she had seen his type before, having spent a good part of her life in saloons. Husbands or boyfriends betrayed by their women and nursing their wounds. So now he was a "type."

"Our next-door neighbor," he said.

"How long has it been going on?"

"I don't know. Maybe it was the first time. But I doubt it."

"Was it your fault or hers?"

He chewed on it for a few seconds before saying, "I guess mine."

"How so?"

"I didn't do my part," he said and immediately realized how foolish that sounded, like they had been engaged in some trivial project. To keep her from probing any deeper, he said, "What about you? You and, uh, Kevin. What happened?"

She took of sip of her wine. "What happened was that two totally fucked-up people ran into each other full speed." She made fists and brought her knuckles together. "We did that until one of us broke." Her clenched hands opened. "That would be me."

She related in a soft, steady voice how her husband had gone bad. The drinking and drugging went from a hobby to a career. He smacked her around when the mood was on him. Of course, there were other women. She laughed crookedly. "I'd call them dumb sluts," she said. "But what would that make me?"

The last straw was the theft of several thousand dollars of the tavern's receipts one night after closing. "And then he disappeared," she said. "Haven't heard from him since. No one has. My dad swore out a warrant for his arrest. But it's been years. Maybe he's in Mexico."

She crushed out her cigarette, got to her feet, and crossed the floor to lean against the window frame opposite Joe. "That's old news," she said. "You're still bleeding here."

Joe wondered what he was supposed to say to that. He didn't want her sympathy. He didn't want to discuss his horrible joke of a Christmas gift. Because the next step might be to pitch himself out the window and be done with it. Though that wasn't his style, either.

Some quiet moments went by. Gina, half in shadow, was regarding him steadily, waiting. He sensed that she would go willingly if he made the slightest move her way. Indeed, as if sensing a change in the air, she turned in his direction. He laid a gentle hand on her shoulder and her response was to raise her head and gaze into his eyes. Her mouth was parted slightly and he knew that if he bent to her, there'd be no turning back. So he wrapped his arm

THE NIGHT BEFORE

around her and pulled her too close to kiss.

She whispered, "Joe. Poor baby."

In the next lingering moments, his mind wandered and he saw himself standing in a series of doorways: the front door of the little frame house he'd grown up in; the one from where he viewed Mariel and Don; finally, the one that opened into Gina's bedroom. His thoughts shifted and he considered the question of one misdeed earning another. Did it matter anymore that he was still married? Having been true to his wife except for a single drunken groping with their neighbor Tina in the front seat of a car five years before, he had never strayed.

Time stretched in an arc that waxed and waned. Gina held fast, purring against him. He was shifting his body against hers when he happened to glance out the window to see a scarecrow standing on the opposite sidewalk, stark and stiff against the new snow.

"There's somebody out there," he said. Peering closer, he saw that it was one of the two customers from Jimmy's. "It's —"

"Sonny." Gina said. "From the bar."

When Joe continued to stare out at the lonely figure, she pulled away from him, turned, and picked up her cigarettes from the end table.

Joe said, "What's he doing out there?"

"What he always does," she said. "Waiting to see if the guy is going to stay."

"What guy?"

In response, she snapped her lighter, blew a slow plume of smoke, and watched it curl to the ceiling.

Joe rubbed the glass, this time with his sleeve. Sonny stood unflinching in the icy breeze that traveled along the street. Joe felt cold just watching him. "How long will he stay there?" he said.

"Until the lights go out." Joe looked at her and she shrugged. "It's what he does."

"Why?"

"Because he thinks he's in love with me."

"Oh. Maybe he is."

"Yeah, maybe," she said.

A quiet minute went by. The glass misted over once more and Sonny disappeared. Gina said, "It's getting late. You should probably go."

Joe tilted his head to the window. "Will you let him come in?"

She gave him a look that was faintly amused. "What do you care?"

"It's Christmas."

"I guess I could."

"I'll tell him, okay?"

She smiled a real smile for the first time all evening. With a slow roll of her eyes, she said, "If you want."

At the door, she surprised him by stretching to kiss his cheek. "Take care of yourself, Joe," she said. "Merry Christmas."

Sonny watched as Joe stopped in the middle of the street. "She says for you to go on up."

Sonny straightened into a posture of uncertainty that he held until Joe had moved off, then made his way to Gina's front door. When Joe looked back, he saw her silhouette at the frosted window above. He raised a hand in farewell, but she didn't see it.

Mariel made her way down the stairs to find that Don had vacated the premises. She went into the kitchen and refilled her glass from the pitcher, hoping to ease the fluttering ache in her chest, but after a small sip of the eggnog, she felt her gut churning again and tossed what was left in the glass down the drain.

She felt shaking weak as she bundled herself for the walk to Betsy's, as if in the wake of a bout of flu. Outside, the sky had cleared, leaving the night crisp and cold, with only an odd flurry crossing her path. After what had just transpired, the familiar street seemed surreal. She recalled the few times in her younger life when she had gotten into real trouble and how she had wished desperately to evaporate, if only to save herself from the wrath of her angry father or the sad face of the boyfriend she had wronged.

Now, as she drew closer to the gay light and happy noise at Betsy's house, she longed for a whirlwind of blowing snow to whip her into oblivion. In a childish moment, she closed her eyes, then opened them again to find that nothing had changed. She was standing at the end of the walk that led to the front door of her friend's house in Eastborough, PA on Christmas Eve, after being caught in the act with her next-door neighbor by her husband of twelve years.

She slowed her steps, entertaining a wild spike of fear that Don had confessed and that Caroline had already shared the tearful news, and she imagined Betsy's living room falling into a silence as the neighbors turned on her, arrayed like a small army of hanging judges, their faces to the man or woman cold and unforgiving. Next, she imagined each one of them holding a stone in a clenched hand...

The bell chimed, the door opened, and she gave a small sigh of relief to be greeted by a wash of music and chatter. Betsy, already buzzed, shrieked her

THE NIGHT BEFORE

name, grabbed her arm, and dragged her into the fray. Someone took her coat and someone else shoved a drink that she didn't want into her hand. She managed a smile and a stream of hellos. The lights in the room were dimmed to reds and greens, which helped obscure her stricken eyes.

She spied Don talking with the Creightons. Caroline was planted at his side, gazing at him with adoring eyes and nodding in earnest over whatever gibberish was coming out of his mouth. He had to be aware that she was in the room, but he wouldn't so much as glance her way. Watching them sidelong, Mariel guessed that they would sweat up the sheets when they got home. Don would make a point of it, as a way to redeem himself.

She rounded the edge of the room and slipped into the kitchen, where she found Karen Sato nibbling from a plate of appetizers. She had always liked Karen, a single mom who seemed to maintain an even keel no matter what crises she faced. Joe was fond of her, too; because she admired his work and because she was voluptuous for an Asian female, and he deeply appreciated the paradox. Or so he said. And Mariel would think: *Right. Pair of what?*

Joe wouldn't know what he was missing this night,

as she was adorned in a gorgeous deep green dress with a plunging neckline. A silver ring on a simple chain rested in her cleavage. The eyes above this display regarded Mariel with concern.

"What's wrong?" Karen placed a hand on her shoulder. "Don't you feel well?" When Mariel shook her head, she said, "Hey. Are you all right?"

"I'm just... I'm..."

Karen leaned closer. "What's wrong?"

Mariel felt a fat tear rise and begin a slow slide down her cheek.

Reverend Callum delivered the two lost souls to St. Mark's A.M.E. Church and drove off in the old van. Though the snow had slowed to flurries, the streets were packed slick and so he maneuvered with care. He longed for some sacred music on the way back to the church, but something was wrong with the wiring under the dashboard and the radio delivered only static. So he made do with the sound of his own mellow voice.

The sky over the city had cleared and the reverend could see stars. The North Star in particular, along with the cold half-moon, seemed to be lighting his path; or perhaps he was just telling himself this was true. The reverend believed deeply in his God, his Savior, and in blessings and miracles, but he was also a rational man who knew the hard ways of the world and was not easily deceived. Not by his own foolishness, and not by the conniving of others.

The two men he had just delivered to the shelter, for instance. One was black, the other white, and both had the look of miscreants. He had collected them at an underpass on I-78 and as soon as they settled into the back seat, they fell to whispers, no doubt trying to decide if the man at the wheel was worth jacking. The reverend put a quick stop to that business, pulling onto the shoulder at Johns Hill and telling them that they could either sit with their mouths closed and their thoughts fixed on the wonder and true meaning of this night, or get out and walk the rest of the way into town.

The pair stared, taking measure of the reverend's thick body and hard eyes and the steel in his voice. They exchanged a glance and decided to heed his advice and enjoy the warm ride. Both shook his hand and thanked him when he delivered them to the shelter. By habit, he checked the seat in case they had left any drugs or weapons. Finding nothing, he wondered if he had misjudged them.

Though he was eager to get back to the church, he took his time, easing to a slow stop at every intersection. He saw only one other vehicle on the streets, an older model Chevrolet that except for a set of flashy chrome wheels was in much the same ragged shape as the van. The car crossed over at Union Street, billowing gray smoke. Reverend Callum drove on.

When the tear erupted into a quiet wail, Karen grabbed Mariel, steered her into the pantry that was just off the kitchen, and closed the door behind them. She pumped her, though gently, and in between the jagged sobs, heard the whole tale: the flirty business with Don that led to heat that turned into fire in their dining room that very night. And how she looked up to see Joe standing in the doorway. The shock on his face! She started to sob again.

"Okay, okay, you need to stop that." Karen waited a moment for her friend to calm herself, then said, "Mariel."

"What?" It came out a comical honk.

"What were you doing with that fool?"

Mariel groaned. "I don't know. It just happened."

"No, it didn't 'just happen.'"

"I guess I was feeling like… like it was all over."

"What was?"

"All of it. Our marriage. All Joe ever does is peck away at some book. He hardly makes any money. He works so hard. But I don't think he's ever going to get anywhere with it."

Karen said, "But he's good with the kids."

"Oh, he's great with the kids. He's just not there with me most of the time. I mean we aren't… I don't know. Anyway, I felt… empty, I guess. Lost. Alone."

"Everybody feels that way sometimes."

Mariel tore a paper towel from the roll on the shelf and dabbed her eyes. "But it passes, doesn't it? I'm not talking about something that goes away when I'm feeling better."

Karen paused for a moment, then said, "Did you want to get caught? Because it was pretty damn dumb. I mean, right there in the house?"

Mariel said, "I don't know. Maybe I did." She sighed and dabbed her nose. "I've been thinking that this is going to be my life. I'll go to work and Joe will sit at that computer and the next thing I know, the kids will be gone and then…"

"And then what?"

"Nothing. That's the point."

Karen said, "And so your answer to this existential dilemma was to screw Don Banks?" Mariel began to weep again. "Okay, okay, I'm sorry. Come on, stop."

Mariel shuddered one time. "I'm all right."

Karen put an arm around her. "You can fix this," she said. "If you want to."

"I don't know…"

"You can try. Right? Mariel?"

"I guess."

"Okay, then." Karen released her. "Ready to face the world?"

Betsy was pulling something from the refrigerator when they stepped out of the pantry. "Hey, you two!" she yelled. "What were you doing in there? Whatever it is, I want in. I'm —" She stopped and produced a bleary look. "Hey, is Joe here? Where is that man?"

Mariel's answer was a sick smile.

Lost in his muddled thoughts, Joe didn't pay attention as block after block went by and the houses changed from common to mean. He passed empty lots and For Rent signs and a series of abandoned cars. The cold wind kicked up as he walked along River Street. The blank silence of the empty homes and storefronts with their boarded-up windows was sad

The Night Before

and just a little creepy. There had once been lives lived in those houses and commerce in the shops. Now it was a ghost town blanketed in white. On another night, he might have been nervous in this part of town, but the snow and Christmas Eve had dampened the traffic. Just to be sure, he bent down to tuck his stack of bills into his sock, keeping a couple twenties in a pocket, a habit left over from his days roaming rough neighborhoods.

Halfway down the next block, he fished out his cell phone and looked at the little screen. Nothing. No missed calls or voice mails and no text messages. No *I'm sorry*. No *Please come home*. No *We miss you*. His gut sank deeper. He punched in the number for the Delaware. After six rings, Melinda answered. He heard music and chatter and wished he wasn't so far away. He asked for Billy.

"Haven't seen him in a couple hours," she said.

"It's Joe Kelly, Melinda."

"Oh, hey, Joe. I'm pretty sure he left."

"He find a Christmas elf?"

"Maybe. I didn't see."

"Okay, well, if you —"

"I'll tell him you called," she said and clicked off.

Joe closed the phone and walked on. From the next

corner, he was able to see the glittering lights on the tallest of the downtown buildings and decided that that was where he needed to be after all. At least a few of the bars would be open, and not the lonesome, dead-end dives like Jimmy's, but places where Christmas Eve stragglers would gather, flush with body heat and happy laughter. Good tunes would be blasting from the speakers over the bar. He'd buy a round for the house, get his back slapped with hearty cheer, and no one would ask what he was doing there.

That's what he needed: a place where he could forget for a little while. He would decide what to do about the rest of the night and the rest of his life later.

Turning back the way he had come, he heard music from a private playlist running through his head. So entranced did he become with a breathless mouthing of half-forgotten lyrics that it took a few seconds for the car coming to an idling stop a half-block behind him to register.

For a brief second, his heart tripped. Had Mariel loaded the kids and come searching for him, as if he was a dog that had gone astray? But then he saw that it was an older model Chevy and not in the best condition. The engine clattered in a rough rhythm and the exhaust smoked with burning oil. In other words, not a vehicle his wife would drive, even if her life and their marriage depended on it.

He caught sight of the Chevy creeping through the intersection ahead and guessed that the driver was lost. Or maybe had been wronged by his or her mate this night and looking for a tender place to land; though looking in the wrong place, to be sure.

He tramped on, turning his thoughts to his book, to certain scenes and the actors who would play the parts in the movie. He knew that an option didn't mean a film would be produced. That was still a long shot — it was Hollywood, after all. And yet what better time for fantasies?

When he reached West Avenue, he saw the Chevy had come to a stop across the intersection, dirty smoke wisping from the tailpipe. At that moment, he felt a buzz in his pocket. He fumbled for a crazy few seconds until he could get the phone out and stare stupidly at the six letters: MARIEL.

He whispered her name. In response, a voice coming from behind made him jump. "You don't need to be takin' no calls right this minute."

Joe turned around to find a man standing there — a kid, actually, in his teens — staring at him from beneath the bill of a baseball cap. He was a few inches shorter than Joe, muscular, with light chocolate skin, a thin nose, and hard green eyes. He wore a new winter coat with the hood pulled up partway. Gold glinted on the lobes of his ears. Both his hands were gloved and one held a buck knife with a glinting blade pointed at Joe's gut.

For the second time in a few short hours, Joe found himself frozen where he stood, in this instance by sheer craziness. This couldn't be happening to him; not on top of his family disaster, and not on this night. His mind traveled to an irrelevancy. What kind of muggers hunted victims on Christmas Eve?

The answer was the sort with partners who drove battered Chevys. Through the blood pounding in his ears, he heard a door creak open with a metallic wince. Another kid, this one taller, thicker, and even younger than the first, stepped up to form a triangle on the lonely corner. He looked excited and scared, his mouth open as he tried to catch his breath.

"Give that fuckin' thing here," the senior partner said, and snatched the phone from Joe's grasp. "Now get out what all's in your pockets." Joe stared at him, unable to connect word to action. "You hear what I said?" the kid barked. "Give it up."

"Okay, okay," Joe said and went fumbling for his wallet.

He had barely drawn it from his pocket when the bigger kid jumped in to grab it. His knife-wielding partner gave him a sharp look, peeved at the break in protocol, then turned back to Joe. "What else you got?"

Joe swallowed, found his voice gone.

"You deaf? I said what else you got, motherfucker?"

Joe held up his hand. "Watch," he said.

The mugger peered, then curled his lip in haughty distaste. "That ain't worth shit. What else?"

His partner flipped Joe's wallet open. "Ain't no cash."

"Where is it?"

"Here," Joe croaked and pointed to his front pocket.

The kid with the knife was watching his eyes. "Get it," he said and Joe felt knobby fingers digging. The younger one stepped back and turned over the bills to his partner.

"That all of it?" his partner said. "You got more, you better give it, man. 'Cause I will cut you up."

The younger kid said, "Wha' 'bout a ring?"

The blade twisted a pattern in front of Joe's face. "Let's see."

Joe pulled off his glove and held up his left hand.

The kid said, "Give it."

Joe startled the two junior criminals by making short work of jerking the wedding band from his finger and slapping it into the knife-wielder's gloved palm. The mugger looked at the ring, looked at him.

"Do you know what tomorrow is?" Joe said.

"It Friday," the younger one spoke up.

His partner shot him a dour look before returning his cold eye to Joe. "We know what the fuck tomorrow is," he said. "It's Christmas. And you're Santa Claus. What else you got?"

"My wife…" Joe said.

The two kids stopped to exchange a glance, their brows stitching.

"Yo' wife?" the one standing before him said. "What the fuck? What about yo' wife?"

"Something happened," Joe said. "At home."

"Somethin' 'bout to happen right here," the kid said, raising the knife a few inches. "I know that ain't all of it."

The young partner stepped up and began slapping Joe's pockets. When one of his hands found the edge of the zebrawood box, Joe flinched and the kid said, "Uh-oh. Whatsat?" He grabbed the shoulder of Joe's coat in one thick paw. "Give it up."

Joe shook his head. "No."

"No? You crazy? You give it up or I'm —"

"Y'all leave the man be."

Three heads turned in a startled second. Reverend Callum stood in the middle of the street, his arms stiff at his sides. Though his eyes glinted like opals, they were steady. The van was parked down the cross street. Neither he nor the two muggers had heard the vehicle or the man approach.

The reverend's studied gaze settled on the kid with the buck knife. "You know who I am?"

The kid's eyes skittered. "Yeah."

"Who am I?"

"Reverend from the church down Iron Avenue."

"That's right. And I know who you are, too. Know where you live. Both y'all. Know your mamas and your grandmamas, all them." He paused to give a slow shake of his head. "And look at y'all out here. Shame on you both."

The kid's eyes and the blade in his hand dipped downward. His partner's face had closed and he joined in fixing his gaze on the snow at his feet. Out of his daze, Joe recognized expressions he knew well. His kids wore those same abashed looks when caught red-handed at something.

"Let go that knife you holding," Reverend Callum said.

The kid made an angry sound and dropped the weapon into the soft snow.

"Now give back whatever you took," the reverend said. The kid didn't move. "Give it back."

A few flakes of snow swirled. The kid heaved a breath, then relented and handed Joe the wallet and phone. For a reason he couldn't fathom, Joe felt ashamed for the boy.

Reverend Callum said, "They take any cash off you?"

"They can keep it." Joe said. He was about to add, "I've got plenty," then thought better of it.

"No," the reverend said. "Those are the rewards of sin."

The kid said something under his breath and held out a stiff hand, the bills folded in his cold fingers. Joe reclaimed the money.

The reverend said, "And whatever else you got." The mugger returned Joe's wedding band. "Now go on. Get in your car, go home, and stay there. It's Christmas Eve."

The two turned away and ambled off in childlike silence.

"And go to church on Sunday," Reverend Callum called out as they crossed the street and climbed into the Chevy. "You two shame your mothers." The car coughed to a start and rattled and smoked down the avenue. The reverend fixed an eye on Joe. "Are you all right, sir?"

Joe, still three moves behind, stared at the reverend, who now stepped up to extend a hand.

"I'm Franklin Callum," he said. "Reverend." He steadied Joe's grip in his own. "It's all right. They're gone. You're lucky they weren't like some of these others."

Joe looked over the reverend's shoulder. He could make out the arc of hand-painted scroll on the side of the van: "The Light of the World" with "Tabernacle" printed in sturdy block letters beneath it.

Reverend Callum said, "What's your name, sir?"

"Joe. Kelly."

"What are you doing out here? You lost?"

"I was…" Joe found his mouth still dry and his stomach churning. "Walking," he said and pointed east. "Downtown."

"That's quite a walk." Reverend Callum peered at Joe with polite interest. "There somewhere I can carry you?"

Joe was befuddled. "I don't know," he said.

The reverend bent to retrieve the knife. With a sigh of regret, he folded the blade and tucked it away. Then he looked at Joe and said, "Well, come on. We can at least get you off this here street."

Slouching in the welcome heat, Joe replayed the mugging in his head. He had gone into a mild state of shock and the reality of the incident was just dawning. It was odd that he hadn't been afraid. In fact, he'd flipped out a little and then got weird. He thought about the looks on the kids' faces when he went off about Mariel and snickered to himself.

The man behind the wheel glanced his way. "You sure you all right?" he said.

"I'm okay." Joe undid the top button of his coat.

"What are you doing out tonight, Reverend?"

"I run a service out of my church for homeless folks and transients," the reverend said. "Find them a place to stay. At shelters and so forth. I'm on my way back from carrying two gentlemen to St. Mark's.

"You don't get to be with your family?"

The reverend's smile moved away. "So happens I don't have any family here," he said. "The church, my congregation, that's my family." They sat in silence for a moment. "And what about you, sir?"

"I live on Crescent Drive. It's up by the college. I have a wife and two kids. And..." And what?

"Crescent Drive?" Reverend Callum said. "Afraid I can't drive you there right this minute. If that's where you're wanting to go, I mean. I got to get back to the church."

"I guess I can call a cab."

"Cab might take you awhile tonight," the reverend said.

"That's all right," Joe said.

"You're welcome to ride in with me. Get wherever you're going from there."

Joe thought for a moment. "I don't know where I'm going."

Reverend Callum produced a curious glance but did not inquire further. He put the shifter into drive and went about manhandling the old van over the snow-laden streets.

"Beautiful when it's like this, ain't it?" he said presently, then began humming a tune in a minor key. Joe leaned his head against the cold glass and watched the dark shapes of buildings that they were passing. The facades of houses and storefronts stared back blankly. Here and there, he saw a string of lights, brave against a bleak frame. Nothing was moving.

Though it wasn't that far to downtown, the warmth and noise and camaraderie of the bars didn't seem so appealing anymore. He yearned to lie down and sleep for a long time. This brought thoughts of the bed that Mariel and he shared, the house, and the kids, and for a moment he felt like he wanted to cry. Instead, he stiffened his jaw and allowed himself a shaky sigh.

The reverend's hummed melody ended on a mellow note. After driving in silence for a block, he said, "Did something happen to you tonight, Mister Joe? I mean along with getting stuck up in here."

"Yeah," Joe said. "Something happened."

"You have a loss?"

"Nobody died, if that's what you mean," Joe said. "Something went wrong. At home."

"On this night?" Callum shook his head gravely. "I'm sorry to hear that."

Joe was tempted to blurt his story to this kind man, to paint the narrative with graphic details, from the thrill of his astonishing success to his grand plan to share it with his wife and kids, arriving at that same wife bent in a lewd posture over their dining room table.

THE NIGHT BEFORE

He only got as far as, "I was…"

"Sir?"

"Nothing," Joe said. "Something happened, that's all. It's over now."

The reverend gazed at him for a final frank moment before returning to the business of pulling the creaking van to the curb in the middle of a quiet and empty block lined with vacant stores and a few ramshackle shotgun houses, all of them dark.

"This is it right here," he said, tilting his head. "You're welcome to step inside, get warm, have a cup of coffee." He wrenched his door open and slid from the seat.

Mariel survived another half-hour of the party by sticking with Karen. They huddled in the kitchen, chatting about this and that, helping with the food and drinks, wandering into the living room just enough to be polite, and avoiding any mention of the night's drama. It was Mariel's good fortune that most of the other neighbors were too sloshed to pay her much mind. Betsy buzzed by to blabber for as long as she could fix her thoughts before careening back to her guests.

As soon as the clock ticked on eleven, Mariel

figured she had done enough and stood at the top of the basement stairs to call down to the kids. She herded them through the crowd and out the front door with a gasp of relief that would have been audible except for all the loud tidings that followed in their wake.

Karen walked with them to the next corner. Pulling up the hood of her coat, she said, "People see me like this, they think I'm a fucking Eskimo."

Mariel shook her head in a forlorn way. She thought Karen looked beautiful and serene, and longed to trade places with her. When they reached the corner, Karen wrapped her in a final hug and whispered, "Call me if you need to," before trudging off down the middle of Leafmore Drive.

Mariel turned around to find Hannah eyeing her in a faintly accusing way, as if she suspected that something was wrong. It would have been no surprise if she did; the girl had always possessed antennae that could pick up the slightest tremor of trouble with either of her parents.

"Where's Dad?" she said and when Mariel failed to produce a snappy reply, turned on a peeved heel and continued on her way.

Mariel felt her heart sink, even as another sob rose

in her throat. They were good children, beautiful children, and did not deserve what was about to be visited upon them. It wasn't fair and it was all her fault. She stood still and bit down hard to keep from coming undone in front of them.

Christian had stopped and was watching her.

"Mom? You okay?"

She didn't move. He and his sister exchanged a glance, then made their way back along the sidewalk. Hannah peered at her with Joe's gray eyes, as if he was playing a long-distance prank on her, one that wasn't funny.

Hannah saw her mother's melancholy smile and touched her arm. "We should go home and wait for him," she said.

The church was a converted storefront of concrete block with a flat roof upon which a sturdy cross had been erected and was now cast in the blue glow of a single spotlight.

Reverend Callum unlocked the front door and held it wide. Joe stepped inside to find six pairs of pews arranged along either side of the small room and facing a low platform with a lectern at its center. The street windows had been covered with patches of colored plastic to emulate stained glass with the odd touch of heavy steel mesh affixed to the frames. A reed organ that appeared to be a relic from the 1960s had been pushed into the corner next to the door through which the reverend now led Joe.

Joe pointed to the windows. "You have to worry about break-ins?" he said.

Reverend Callum said, "About what? Oh. Yes, sir. Desperate people will do wrong, even at a church. These things happen. But don't worry. We're safe here."

He led his guest into an office in the back of the building. It was as tidy as a space cramped with two desks, several sets of bookshelves, a credenza, a folding cot made up to military precision, and a trio of file cabinets could be. The lamps on each desk cast the room in shades of amber. A Christmas hymn played softly from an old radio in fake wood grain that was perched atop one of the file cabinets.

Reverend Callum dropped his gloves and keys and waved a hand to the desk in the corner. "Have a seat," he said. "Warm yourself." He peered at the telephone. "No calls," he murmured. "That's good. Thank God."

He began puttering about his desk, shuffling papers.

Joe settled into the chair and as the music whispered kindly from the radio, he rested his head on his folded arms and closed his eyes. An image of his house drifted into his mind, a postcard blown on a breeze, the outside lights glowing against the fallen snow and the tree that took up a whole corner of the front room visible through a misty window. Though a pleasant portrait, it seemed strange, as if from a foreign place. How odd it was that he would feel that way after so much time?

In the next frame, his children's sweet faces appeared at the window and he felt a dark chill run through his bones, a sudden sickening notion that one or both weren't his. Whose, then? Don's? Some other long ago lover's? Who knew how many there had been over there twelve years? He felt panic rise in his chest, his heart thumping so hard that he could —

"Mister Joe?"

Reverend Callum was standing before him, his brow stitched in concern. "You all right? You were making some noise over here."

Joe raised his head, blinking blearily. "Sorry. I dozed off."

The reverend was holding two butter cookies on a napkin in one hand and a cracked coffee cup in the other. "Thought you might like a little something," he said.

Joe stared at the offering for a long moment. "Thank you." He accepted the snack and went about nibbling and sipping, as dutiful as a child.

The reverend stood back to regard him in a pensive way. He said, "You want me to call you a cab? Or you got some friend or family you want to come collect you?"

Joe thought about it. Mariel had not left a message on his cell phone and he wasn't ready to talk to her anyway. He could try Billy again, but phoning a noisy saloon from such a hallowed place seemed somehow profane. Also, he still wasn't sure he wanted his best friend to know of this night's shame. So he said, "I'll just stay for a while, if you don't mind."

"Don't mind at all," Reverend Callum said. "You're welcome here." He ambled to his desk, sat down, and opened an old Bible, its spine broken and pages frayed.

Joe finished his cookies, aware of the reverend lifting his eyes from the scripture to glance his way, no doubt pondering what sort of tribulations had landed him on the cold Eastborough streets on Christmas Eve in the first place.

He imagined himself saying: *I caught my wife. With our next-door neighbor. Caught them right as I was about to share the best news that's come my way in years. That was God's gift to me this night, Reverend.*

The words remained unspoken and he pushed past a replay of the dining room scene. Now his brain switched to another show, this one featuring Don and Mariel and the kids from both households thrown together into one big happy family. (Joe and Caroline having been put out on the curb for pickup.) The new couple's combined incomes would add up to serious money and the kids would have everything they ever wanted, every day. Caroline would go directly into spinsterhood and Joe would end up drinking himself to death on his movie money, a shaking wreck of a —

The phone jangled, jerking him out of the nightmare. Reverend Callum lifted the receiver, listened, spoke a few quiet words. He dropped the phone back in the cradle and stood up.

"You ain't in any hurry to leave?" he asked.

Joe shook his head.

"Then you mind watching the phone while I go collect someone?"

Joe said, "I can do that."

The reverend took his coat down from the hook on the wall. Joe followed him into the chapel.

"What happens if someone calls?" he said.

"Ain't too likely that'll happen this late," Callum told him. "But just go ahead and get their location. If they're outside, tell them to get indoors or under shelter and call back in just a bit. Tell them I'll be around soon as I can." He was buttoning his coat. "I won't be gone but twenty-five, thirty minutes." He stepped out into the night and locked the door behind him.

Joe peered through a tear in one of the pieces of colored plastic. It had begun snowing again, though lightly, barely dusting what was already on the street. He watched the reverend climb in behind the wheel. The van stuttered off into the night trailing a billow of gray smoke.

Except for the reedy music from the office radio, the little church was quiet. Joe moved from the window and sat down in a front pew. He noticed that the cross on the wall behind the pulpit was made of a hardwood he didn't recognize, the color of honey, but swirled with bands of deep black grain. It was starkly stirring, constructed in a way that announced an imperfect hand. Reverend Callum's? It would not surprise him to find out that the cross was the preacher's work.

Sitting there, he admitted to himself that he had taken advantage of that kind man's errand to linger and avoid a decision. It was also true that there was nowhere he cared to go. A cab could carry him to a hotel downtown or a motel out on the interstate. He imagined greeting Christmas morning alone in an empty and antiseptic room while the rest of the world celebrated. Hannah and Christian would come downstairs to find him absent. What story would Mariel tell them? He couldn't imagine; he was the one with all the grand fiction.

Crashing at Billy's or his parents' or one of his siblings' was out of the question. No, he would be home for his children on Christmas morning. No matter what happened afterward. The thought cheered him until he began mulling what he'd say to Mariel when he saw her again. As for the kids, he'd concoct something. The carload of presents would distract them for a while. And he would make a point of announcing the news about the option and the money that was coming their way. He took a moment to picture Mariel's face when she realized that she had picked the wrong time to destroy the family.

It was no good. Such imaginings wearied him and seemed a frankly cruel fit on someone taking grateful refuge in that sanctuary for the soul.

He turned back to wondering how much he could blame Mariel for what had happened. That he had never in his life committed a truly horrible act didn't make him an innocent. She'd had every right to expect more from him and he had let her down. If for a certain actor stumbling on his book, nothing would have changed. That it had been so close a call was a humbling notion.

It was in this chastened mood that he rose from the pew and ambled back into the office to call home to make some kind of arrangement. Standing over the telephone, he hesitated, preparing a speech. It wouldn't do to lose his temper. Cool and calm, he told himself. No shouts or curses or name-calling and no breaking down. Just get into it and see where they stood.

He was still working on his opening line when the phone chattered. There was an urgency to the ring tone that caused him to snatch up the receiver. "This is the... the Light of the World." He stuttered over the words. *The Light of the World?*

Background noise and someone talking crowded a

THE NIGHT BEFORE

female voice. "This the shelter place?"

Joe said, "This is the church, yes. Can I help you?"

"We got put out." The woman sounded a bit hoarse.

"Put out?"

"Put out on the street," she said. "Malikah and me. We need help. Some place to stay."

Joe said, "I'm not —"

"Hello?"

"Yes, ma'am. I'm here."

"I got my child with me. She's only seven."

Joe rubbed his forehead with the back of his hand. "Where are you?"

"Store on Butler Street. Corner of Sixth."

"I'm sorry, I can't —"

"Can't what?" The other voice muttered in the background. "The man says we need to leave."

"I'm sorry? What man?"

"The manager here."

Joe stared at the wall, feeling something come over him.

The woman said, "Hello?"

"Put him on the phone."

Clattering sounds were followed by a voice with a South Asian lilt. "Yes? May I help you?"

"This is Joe Kelly." He reached for a tone of authority even as he ad-libbed the script. "I'm with the Light of the World Tabernacle."

The voice came back, now more cautious. "Yes, sir?"

"You're the manager of the store?"

"The night manager, yes, sir."

"Well, a happy holiday to you."

"And the same to you, sir."

"I need to ask a favor. The woman and her child are not causing a problem, are they?"

"Problem?" The manager hesitated. "No, sir."

"Then can you let them stay until I can get someone there?"

"Sir?"

"Somebody will come to get them. From the church. It's below freezing outside. And it's Christmas Eve. We would appreciate it."

"And how long must they stay?"

"No more than a half-hour."

"Oh…" The manager paused. "All right, then. Very good."

"Butler at Sixth, right?"

"That's right, yes, sir."

"Thank you. Can I speak to the woman?"

The phone was passed back. "Hello?"

"He's going to let you stay. Someone will come get you and your child. Probably the... Reverend Callum. He's out on a call right now."

"Okay, then. Thank you."

"What's your name?"

"Nicole. Weaver."

"I'm Joe."

"Okay, then."

"You stay put, all right?"

The woman said, "We ain't going anywhere. Got nowhere to go."

With that, she clicked off. Joe dropped the phone in the cradle, then hurried into the chapel and poked his nose to the mesh-framed window. The van was not in sight.

He stood wondering if he was being touched by a stroke of magic. But such events didn't really happen, did they? Except in movies and books, of course. What did happen was that a decent man who'd been a lifelong disappointment to himself and his family and friends came home with great news for the first time in forever only to find his wife coupled with the next-door neighbor, who happened to be a genuine prick.

Searching the street for headlights, he pulled his mind off his own problems and thought about the woman and child in need of a refuge on this frigid night. If the reverend wasn't back in the next fifteen minutes, he'd have to try and call a cab to pick them up. But the woman wouldn't have money to pay the driver. He wondered if they took credit cards over the phone. He was so absorbed in this happy confusion that it took a few seconds for the crunch of a metal door closing to register.

He was waiting when Reverend Callum stepped inside. "I got a call," he said. "A woman was put out of her house. She's at a convenience store on Butler Street. She has a kid with her. A little girl."

The reverend unbuttoned his coat. "Little girl? Oh, my."

Joe followed him into the office. "The manager told her they had to leave," he said. "I talked him into letting them stay. Only for a half-hour, though." Callum sat down at his desk. "So, can you go get her?"

Reverend Callum stood at his desk to regard Joe for an absent moment, as if something else was occupying his thoughts. The announcer on the radio whispered that they were coming up on the midnight hour. The reverend smiled in a vague way at Joe's fidgeting, then lifted his ring of keys from the desk, and dangled them in the air.

"Why don't you go?" he said.

The van was a creaking hulk to drive. The engine wheezed and the suspension hobbled over the snow-crusted streets. But the heater blew mightily.

Joe steered his careful way west through town. The last thing he wanted was to end up wrapped around a pole and have the poor woman and her child waiting there, thinking he had abandoned them on this of all nights.

It was right on top of the hour when he turned onto Butler Avenue and spied the lights of the store. The street lay dark and quiet under the blanket of snow. He swung into the lot, came to a stop next to a bank of pay phones, and cut off the lights. The wipers swept the windshield a last time and he saw the little girl gazing out at him from the other side of the glass with the kind of patience that only a child can muster — steady and without a hint of guile. She watched him climb out of the van and she stood motionless as he raised a gloved hand to wave at her.

He pushed through the glass door, nodded a greeting to the short, dusky man inside the glass booth, and turned down the first aisle. The woman didn't rush at him in a desperate lunge. Instead, she drew her daughter to her side and stood somewhat stiffly against the backdrop of merchandise, as if waiting for a proper introduction. She was dark-skinned and too thin. Her face was made of sharp planes and there was something proud in her steady gaze and the tilt of her chin. Her hair was wound in braids and streaked with gold and her eyes were wide and deep, black pools.

Joe was relieved to see that the little girl looked healthy, with chubby cheeks at both ends of a shy smile. Her eyes were enormous and full of light and he was charmed.

Catching himself, he offered the mother his hand. "Nicole? I'm Joe. I'm the one you talked to."

"Yes, sir." Her fingers felt cold.

Joe smiled at the little girl. "And what's your name?"

"Malikah." It was just above a whisper.

"Okay," he said and clapped his hands. "I guess we're ready."

He herded them to the front of the store, where he stopped to wave through the bulletproof glass at the manager. Malikah slowed her steps to cast her wide eyes upon the display of cookies and cakes on the end cap.

Joe said, "Would you like something?" He looked at her mother. "Is it all right?" Nicole nodded and he said," Go ahead. Pick whatever you want."

Joe and the manager traded a smile as the child agonized. After a moment, Joe leaned down to whisper, "You can pick two. One for now, one for later." He turned to the mother. "And what about you? Please, get something."

Nicole's face softened at this kindness and studied the display of pastries wrapped in plastic.

Joe said, "Malikah. You like chocolate milk?" The child nodded gravely. "Okay. What about you, ma'am? A Coke or…?"

Nicole said, "Coke's fine," and Joe made a quick tour, returning with the drinks. His spirits were in a dizzy spin as he helped count the purchases and then pay. He thanked the clerk and wished him a happy holiday for the second time.

Nicole got Malikah strapped into the back seat, then settled in front. Joe climbed in behind the wheel, cranked the engine, and turned on the heater. Plastic crinkled as Malikah attacked the first of her snacks.

Nicole was blinking at the snowflakes, her brow furrowing. "Where you taking us?"

Joe had forgotten about that. He dug for his phone, then got out to read the number splayed on the side of the van. The reverend answered in his slow drawl. Joe reported that he had collected the mother and daughter as he climbed back into the driver's seat.

"You can go ahead and carry them to St. Mark's A.M.E. on Farwick Avenue," the reverend said. "You know where that is? Almost down to Sage?"

"I can find it," Joe said.

"I called over and spoke to Mrs. Walters. She runs the shelter. They got beds for the two of them. So go ahead and carry them there and then bring the van on in."

Joe clicked off and told Nicole where they were going. She and Malikah exchanged whispers. He said, "Something wrong?"

"We got to go back and get our things," the mother said.

"Back where?"

"To where we were staying. It's on Grant Street."

"What's there?"

"Our clothes and stuff." Malikah whispered something that Joe didn't catch. "And her presents.

She has Christmas presents."

Joe turned and saw the blades of worry in the child's eyes. She was holding her lip tight to keep from crying. He knew the look.

"Where is it?" he said.

Joe was not waiting at the house. Though Mariel hadn't expected him, it was another small blow. She closed the door. Hannah and Christian moved across the living room, doffing their coats, winding down.

At the bottom of the steps, Hannah called "Dad?" She looked at her mother. "Where is he?"

"It's a surprise. Something he's been working on." The words were out of Mariel's mouth before she could stop them. She knew she had just dug herself a deeper hole, but she was too tired to think of anything else. Hannah and Christian exchanged a glance, wondering if their dad might be planning one in a series of stunts that were amusing only to him. When that happened, there was nothing to do but play along and hope it wasn't too lame. They wished Mariel a good night and trundled up the stairs.

She stood by the front window, peering out onto the white street. Joe was too good a father to not be there when his children awoke on Christmas morning. She hadn't let herself think of a darker reason why he hadn't appeared. He had never been good at avoiding trouble. On this night, after what he had seen, who knew what might have happened after he wandered out? She wondered if it was possible that the tragedy could get worse. And then what would she tell the children? They would never forgive her and it would be her cross to bear forever.

In the next moment, she thought about him wandering in the night and said a small prayer for his safety. Please, she whispered to the cold glass. *Let him come home. His children are waiting.*

The street outside lay still and silent and she felt a chill of fear that something else would go terribly wrong before the night was over.

Grant Street ran through a neighborhood populated by rundown frame houses that even the fresh coating of snow couldn't make over. Only a few of the residents of the narrow avenues had bothered with Christmas lights. Joe didn't see a single new car and some of the vehicles appeared to have been sitting for so long they had become monuments.

"It's down along here," Nicole told him. Joe saw the way her eyes glinted in the dark.

THE NIGHT BEFORE

The mother and daughter began an exchange of animated whispers as they drove along the street and Joe understood that the child was fretting over the fate of gifts that had been left behind. Her soft pleas irked Nicole to the point that she cut off the discussion with a curt word. A half-block further on, she nodded in a tense way and said, "This is it."

Joe pulled over and shut off the engine.

Nicole said, "We'll be back in just in a minute."

Joe saw something stark in her expression and said, "You want me along?"

She shook her head. "No, it'll be fine." She didn't sound too sure.

"Who's in there?"

Nicole was staring the curtained window. "Man I been staying with," she said. "His mama's in there, too. It's her house." Before Joe could inquire further, she said, "Okay, let's get this done," and opened the door.

If the radio had been working, he might have missed the commotion starting. He watched Nicole grip Malikah's hand and they made their way down the slick walk and then up the front porch steps. They went missing in the shadows for a half minute and Joe was about to get out and ask if there was something wrong when the door opened in a sudden spill of blue television light. Mother and daughter disappeared inside.

He twiddled the radio dial, received nothing but static, and had just switched it off when a squall erupted from inside the house, sharp and angry and loud enough to reach his ears. He rolled down the window as a man's voice joined the woman's, whining out a plea. Over the top came Nicole's hard soprano. In a matter of seconds, the three voices wound to a shrill pitch.

Joe climbed out and stepped around the front of the van, reaching the sidewalk as the door banged open in a second wash of pale blue. There were more angry shouts and then two adults and a child tumbled onto the porch in a clutter of shrieks and waving arms.

Malikah escaped down the steps first, shaking and sobbing as she jerked a plastic garbage bag that was too big for her over the snow. Her mother backed away from the door. A man's figure followed. Voices flared once more, his whine against her hard snap. The noise roused the neighbor next door and the light came on one porch over, illuminating the couple in pale yellow.

The man was begging Nicole not to leave. She hoisted a bag of her own in one hand and held out the free one to warn him off, then turned and descended the steps. The man came after her and had just reached the sidewalk when an old woman lurched into the doorway, a jagged silhouette.

"Terry!" The voice was thick, an angry rasp. "Get back in here!"

Terry didn't mind her, tottering behind Nicole in his stocking feet. "Nikki," he moaned. "Malikah. Please. Don't go." Tears streaked his pale cheeks as he hobbled along.

The woman screeched from the porch. "I don't want that bitch and her brat near this house no more! Terry! You hear me?"

Malikah reached the van, sobbing. Joe lifted the bag from her grasp and loaded it and her into the back seat. Nicole was a dozen steps behind and he took her bag, tossed it in back, and closed the door. She climbed into the passenger seat, pushed down the lock, and stared straight ahead, her eyes brittle. Terry stumbled along the sidewalk, still babbling pleas. Joe knew the signs and the guy had junkie written all over him: thin as a rail, sallow-faced and unkempt, in a dirty t-shirt even in that cold. A scrawl of tattoos ran down both arms.

Joe was blocking his path and Terry shot him a bitter glance, his mouth turned downward as if stitched in place.

"Who the... who the fuck is that?" He stopped to peer at the script on the side of the van, his lips moving as he read the words. "The Light of the..." He took Joe in with one harsh glance. "I asked who the fuck are you." His voice broke high and raw. "What are you doin' here? This ain't none of your goddamn business."

"Yeah, it is." Joe raised a gloved hand, fingers splayed. "Now back up," he said. "Leave it be."

Terry's wet eyes flared and he sputtered out a curse. With a jerking motion, he tried to slap the hand aside and make a move for Nicole's door.

Joe didn't realize that he had slammed him with a forearm to the chest until he heard the slap of a body landing on the sidewalk and a woof of breath. Sprawling on the shiny snow in his dirty t-shirt, the poor junkie appeared as shocked as Joe was to find himself there. He let out another curse and began to scrabble to his feet.

Joe heard a stranger bark, "I'll knock you out," and in the next second, realized that it was his voice and his arm cocked with the fist clenched tight.

Terry's eyes went wide at the violence in his tone and he had the sense to stay on his knees. The old woman had hobbled to the porch banister and now leaned over, displaying the splotched, burnt-down face of a dedicated boozer as she swayed up to grip the rail for support. She waved a flabby arm at Joe.

"Leave your hands off him, you!" It came out a drunken slur. "And get that bitch away from here! Else I'm calling the police." She fixed an inflamed eye on her son. "Terry, you get the hell back in the house. I mean now, goddamnit!"

Terry rose shakily to his feet and began to weep again, his bony shoulders heaving. Joe backed around the front of the van and climbed in behind the wheel. He could feel the eyes of the mother and child on him as he slid into the seat. He said, "Okay, we're okay," and then said it again. With the words came a bitter taste on the back of his tongue. His heart was running in overdrive and his stomach twisted and heaved. He had been ready to take Terry apart, tear up his poor junkie ass right there on the sidewalk. His fingers trembled so much that it took two tries to get the key into the ignition and crank the engine.

Terry stood gaunt in the glare of the headlamps.

Nicole stared out the window, her face a ghostly mask. Malikah whimpered softly in the back seat.

Joe pulled out. When they passed under the streetlight at the next corner, he glanced over at Nicole and saw a tear glisten in her eye.

He said, "Are you okay?"

She nodded. He peeked in the mirror. Malikah was huddled down in her coat, cuddling her stuffed alligator as if it could save her from drowning. Though her eyes were brilliant in the darkness.

Joe felt like he had to say something. "Malikah? You know it's not right to hit people, okay? To solve problems that way?" His voice sounded odd and weak in the tinny silence, but it was all he had.

"She knows," Nicole whispered. "Can we please go?"

They covered the ten blocks in about that many silent minutes and arrived at St. Mark's. The square, two-story brick building was unlit save for one basement window. Nicole, Malikah, and Joe stared at it, a trio of dubious faces, two brown, one white.

Joe had managed to calm himself. "Okay, then," he said and grabbed the door handle.

Malikah said, "Mama?"

Nicole said, "It's just for tonight." They were the first words she had spoken since Grant Street and they came out sounding weary.

Joe helped Malikah hoist her plastic bag to the curb. They circled the church to the basement steps on the back side. He rang the bell. He smiled at Malikah as they waited in the cold. "What's your alligator's name?" he said. She clutched the animal tighter and didn't answer, burying her face into her mother's coat. The door opened and a broad, black-skinned woman with thick glasses perched on her nose looked the curious trio up and down.

Joe said, "Are you Ms. Walters?"

"Yes, sir."

"Reverend Callum from the Light of the World called you?"

"Yes, sir, he did," the woman said. She eyed them for another moment before standing back. "Come on in."

She led them down a dark hallway that was adorned with children's drawings of Christmas and at the end of the hall, opened double doors on a large room. Thirty cots were arranged in neat rows, each one occupied by a sleeping form.

"Over here in the corner," Mrs. Walters whispered

and motioned for them to follow her. They skirted the wall to the end of the row and the only two empty beds.

Malikah said. "Mama, I want to go home."

A woman on the next cot raised herself on an elbow. "People tryin' to sleep here," she crabbed.

"It's all right," Mrs. Walters said.

The woman continued to stare.

Malikah said, "Mommy?"

Nicole came up with a sharp look of her own and held it until the woman laid down again. She dropped her bag onto the cot behind her. "We'll be okay," she said.

Mrs. Walters had collected a clipboard from a narrow table along the wall and handed it to Nicole with instructions on how to complete it. Once she finished her spiel, she cocked an eyebrow at Joe, as if surprised to find him still standing there. She said, "Thank you, sir," in a pointed way.

Joe found Nicole's face blank. She said, "We'll be all right now," and managed a small smile. "Thank you for your help."

Joe bent slightly and said, "Good-bye, Malikah. And Merry Christmas." She gave him a searching look, but said nothing.

He ducked into a doorway a few paces down the hall and dialed the church. The phone rang six times before an answering machine picked up and the reverend's deep, rusty voice reported that he had stepped away and would be back directly.

Joe clicked off. Standing in the shadows, he could hear gruff mutterings from inside the large room. A child whimpered briefly and someone coughed. The corridor smelled of an acrid cleanser. He crept back to the doors. Peering through the safety glass, he could make out the mother and child perched side-by-side on the cot. Malikah was curled against her mother, who was in the process filling out the form on the clipboard with slow motions of the pen. It made Joe tired just to watch her.

He saw bags and suitcases in haphazard stacks about the room. It looked so bleak and he wondered if everyone would be allowed to stay tomorrow. Would they flush them out onto the streets on Christmas Day? Could that be? He conjured an image of Nicole and Malikah wandering the cold sidewalks, the child clutching her bag of gifts in a small, stubborn hand.

He stepped away from the doors, tried the number at The Light of the World once more and got the answering machine again. When he returned to push his face to the glass, he found the quiet scene skewed. The woman who had hissed at Malikah was sitting up again. Nicole was on her feet and Malikah was cowering behind her. The two women were locked on each other and there was no mistaking their angry profiles.

Joe pushed the doors open. As he cut through the maze of beds, he heard them spitting curses at each other. Some of the other women sat up, awakened by the noise. Mrs. Walters was moving in on the fray from her desk in the corner.

Malikah saw Joe, grasped her mother's sleeve, and said, "Mama?"

Nicole pulled her eyes off the woman on the cot. With a deft move, Joe stepped between the combatants and held Nicole gently by the arm. "I don't think you should stay here," he said.

Mrs. Walters bustled up, put a hand on her hip, and addressed Joe. "I need for you to leave," she said. "I'll take care of this." She treated the woman on the cot to a fierce glare. "You be quiet and go back to sleep. I mean now." She turned to Nicole. "And you got to finish with the form, ma'am. You ain't registered 'til you're done with that."

"Go where?" Nicole said.

Ms. Walters tapped Joe's shoulder with a crooked finger. "Sir?" she said. "You got to leave. Right this minute."

"I'll find someplace else," he said. "Reverend Callum... I mean, he and I will. We'll help you."

She was watching him with dark, uncertain eyes. Malikah huddled at her side.

"Sir!" Mrs. Walters said. "Do I need to call security?"

Joe said, "Please."

Nicole stood still for a few seconds. She said, "You don't need to call anyone, ma'am," and gathered her daughter with one hand and her suitcase with the other.

Ms. Walters tracked them down the hall on slippers with broken backs. She was having trouble keeping up as Joe, Nicole, and Malikah made their getaway, but she managed, propelled by a rising ire.

"You don't need to be doing this," she fumed. "I can take care of any trouble. You hear me?"

Joe hustled Malikah and Nicole ahead of him. "I heard you, yes, ma'am."

The woman was losing her temper. "This ain't a hotel. You know I got to call Reverend Callum. He ain't going to like it one bit."

Joe said, "I'll explain it." They had reached the street door. "Thank you for your courtesy."

He hurried Malikah and Nicole out into the cold night. Mrs. Walters's lips were drawn tight as she closed the door hard behind them. The clack of the lock echoed down the empty street.

Nicole let Malikah lead the way back to the van. She took a moment to draw close to Joe, drop her voice, and say, "You better not be up to something."

He stopped and looked at her. "Like what?"

Her eyes slid his way. "You know what I mean."

"I'm not up to anything," he said. "I'm taking you back to the reverend's church. Okay?"

Though her mother's face remained closed, Malikah's eyes were bright again as she clambered into the van. "Where are we going?" she said.

"Someplace nice," Joe told her. "It's called 'The Light of the World.'"

He cranked the engine and made a U-turn in the middle of the street. The vents sent out a blast of heat and Nicole loosened her coat. Joe saw that her face was softer in the blue of the dashboard lights.

He said, "Don't worry, it's going to be fine," and she nodded.

The Night Before

A lonely tree with a few thin strings of lights glowed from a window of a house they were passing. Joe glanced in the mirror and said, "Malikah? Do you know any Christmas songs?"

The child cocked her head. "Mama does."

"Mama does?" Joe looked over at Nicole, who shook her head slightly and gave up a small sand shy mile.

"And she sings good, too," Malikah said. "Sing, mama."

"No..."

Joe said, "Come on. I'd like to hear."

Nicole waved the two of them off with a shy hand and fixed her gaze on something above the rooftops. Joe had just about given up when she began, starting low then rolling up to fill the van with a sweet contralto.

Fall on your knees, O hear the angel voices
O night divine, O night when Christ was born
Oh night divine, O night, O night divine...

By the fourth note, Joe had lifted his foot from the gas and turned to gape in wonder over the sounds from her slender throat. The tones were honeyed and while there was something anguished about the way the song poured out of her, there was also no denying that it was lifted on hope. When the last echo died, she noticed the astonishment on his face and said, "I sang in the choir back home."

She turned away and began to croon the melody. Joe listened, feeling an ache in his chest. Miles away, his house sat warm and quiet, with the lights from the tree filling the front window. The kids would be in their beds by now, though he knew Christian would have a hard time settling down.

He wondered if they had asked their mother why he wasn't home and imagined Mariel trying to put on a front. She'd have to lie, of course. Could she get away with it? The kids were sharp, his daughter especially. She'd know something was wrong and would worry. He went back to cursing his wife for the betrayal, the act itself and the stupidity of letting herself get caught. On Christmas Eve, no less. She was —

"Hey."

The final hummed note had faded and they were idling at an intersection. Joe looked at Nicole and then peered into the mirror. Mother and child were regarding him with matching vexed expressions. Something had gone terribly wrong in their lives, too. Indeed, compared to what had befallen them, his drama seemed a frivolous thing. They had been tossed from a rude home onto a cold street with nowhere to go. He pondered the odd set of turns that had brought them together on this night, amidst the first Christmas Eve snowfall in seven years.

"Something wrong with the van?" Nicole said.

He returned to the moment. "No, it's okay. I just..." They rolled forward. "It's down the next street."

Reverend Callum opened the door. His liquid eyes were cool but he said nothing as Nicole, Malikah, and Joe filed inside.

Joe made the stuttering introductions. No one seemed to know what to do next and before it got strange, he said, "Reverend, do you have anything in your office that a seven-year-old girl might enjoy?"

The cheap ploy worked. The reverend pulled his gaze off Joe and pursing his lips and furrowing his forehead in a clownish arc, he fixed wide eyes on Malikah.

"I don't guess you mean cookies and milk," he said. "Naw. You don't like cookies, do you?" Malikah nodded gravely. "You do? Well, all right, then. Come on this way."

He ushered the three of them into his office. The radio gurgled sweetly as he went about opening a box of Oreos and producing a carton of milk from the refrigerator. Joe drew a cup of coffee from the pot on the side table for Nicole.

He dropped his voice to say, "Can you wait in the chapel while we talk?"

Nicole said, "Malikah, come with mama." They walked out of the office and Joe closed the door behind them.

Reverend Callum was abrupt. "What's this about? I got a phone call from Mrs. Walters. She wasn't happy. You abused her hospitality. Why'd you do that?"

"I'm sorry, I didn't —" Joe said. "I couldn't —"

"Couldn't what?"

"I didn't want to leave them in that place. Not tonight."

"It's a shelter," the reverend said. "What it's there for."

"I know. I just…" He caught a breath and told him about the house on Grant Street, the boyfriend and her mother, and the dreary space at the church, the nasty woman on the next cot.

Reverend Callum listened, then shook his head.

"Should have left them there anyway," he said. "Now what are you going to do? They can't stay here."

"I know, I know," Joe said. "I'll find them a hotel, I guess."

"And then what?"

"Then what?"

The reverend's face darkened. "You one of these damn do-gooders, sir?" His rumbling tone turned harsh. "You stick yourself in someone else's business and then get all proud 'cause you did them some little favor? So you can feel good at Christmas time? 'Course, the rest of the year, you ain't nowhere to be found. You one of them?"

Joe felt his face burning. "No, I — nothing like that."

Callum regarded him with a faint contempt. "You think you were just going to dump them on me, now that you played the hero? Why you want to do something like this?" He stretched his arm and pointed a heavy finger in the direction of the chapel. "That's a child out there."

"I'm going to deal with it," Joe said.

Reverend Callum tilted his head, as solemn as a judge. "That's right, you are," he said. "'Cause you ain't got a choice now. Not if you're any kind of a man."

The arm came down. Joe dropped his head, mortified at his foolishness. After a moment, Reverend Callum's gaze calmed, along with his tone. "Ain't like I ain't seen it before, son. Seen people do like this, I mean."

"Yes, sir, I understand." Joe felt the guilt settling on him. "I'm sorry."

"I'm sure you are," the reverend said.

"I wanted to…"

"To what?"

"Get my mind off what happened. Before, I mean."

Now the reverend treated him to an inquisitive look. "And what did happen?"

"Something at home. With my wife." Joe hoped that he wouldn't have to explain.

Well, whatever it was, I'm sorry," the reverend said. "But it don't matter. What matters right now is that woman and her baby."

Joe said, "I'll take care of them. I will." The reverend's face remained passive. "I'm going to go talk to her. We'll figure something out."

He had only gone a few steps when Reverend Callum said, "Son?" Joe stopped. "You can dump them on me if you need to. Just don't make it worse."

"I won't," Joe said. "And I won't."

THE NIGHT BEFORE

When he opened the door to the chapel, what he saw caught and held him there. Nicole was sitting in the front pew, holding a sleeping Malikah across her lap. The light was low and had a golden cast that seemed to envelop them. It was a sweet picture. He thought the mother was also asleep until he stepped closer and she raised her head. He sat down next to her and they both watched Malikah doze. The child's face was angelic.

"I remember my kids when they were that age," he said.

"How old are they now?" Nicole said.

"Nine and ten."

"Where they at?"

"At home with their mom." He paused, pushing aside the picture that seeped into his mind. "I want you to know I'm going to help you out here. Find a place for you to stay, I mean."

"Why?"

"Why? Because... because I'm the one who came and got you. And I took you out of the shelter. So I think I should. I want to."

Nicole didn't speak, studying him closely, and he figured she was waiting for the catch.

He said, "I'm guessing you can't go back to your house."

"Won't," she said, and swallowed. "Don't want to."

Joe turned slightly to face her. "What were you doing with him?"

She took a long moment before saying, "I met him in rehab. I had a drug problem. Me and him both did. He was funny. Always made me laugh. So after we got out, I saw him some more." She paused. "I lost our apartment and so we moved into the house with him and his mama. It would have been fine. If it wasn't for her. And his dope." She sighed. "Anyway, we ain't goin' back. You heard that old bitch." She shook her head. "He wouldn't ever stand up to her. But he cared for Malikah. He sure did. When he could."

They were quiet for a few moments. Joe said, "So do you still...?"

"Have the drug problem? I'll always have that. I'm an addict." She raised her chin. "But I'm clean eleven months now. And I'm staying that way." She gazed down at her sleeping child again. "I have to."

She fixed him with a speculative eye and said, "What about you? What are you doing out tonight?

Y'all Jewish?"

"We're not anything," Joe said. "I, uh… she…" He paused to collect himself. "Something really amazing happened to me in the last couple weeks," he said. "I got some money I wasn't expecting. Not a lot, but not a little, either. And so I wanted to surprise them with it. My wife and the kids. For Christmas. For once."

"What's her name?"

"Mariel." It sounded odd to his ear, as if he was talking about a stranger. "Anyway, I went out and bought presents for the kids and I found something that she wanted a long time ago. Back when we were first married."

"What kind of something?"

He patted his pockets until he located the zebrawood box, then opened it and drew out the jewel on its thin chain. "It's called an Epiphany Star."

Nicole studied the multi-colored gems. "It's pretty. Looks old."

"It is."

"Cost you a lot, huh?"

"It wasn't —" He paused. She was regarding him wisely.

"Okay, so you bought it for her," she said.

"And I carried it home. With the bank statement, showing the money we had now. I was going to make this big surprise." He entertained the strange notion that Nicole knew what was coming. "And when I got to the house, I found her with another man."

Nicole stopped and stared. "Uh-oh. What other man?"

"Our next-door neighbor."

"Were they…"

"Oh, yes," Joe said.

"In your bed?"

"In the dining room."

"The dining room?

Joe nodded. "Over the table." He chased the image with a shake of his head.

"Well, damn. What'd you do?"

"I left. Wandered half the night. Ran into Reverend Callum. And ended up here."

Malikah sighed in her sleep. Nicole smiled down at her in a kindly absent way. "That's some story," she said. "Christmas Eve, too." She regarded him thoughtfully for a moment. "So what are you gonna do now?"

Joe slumped against the back of the pew. "I have no idea."

"Your kids gonna be waiting for you."

He said, "Yeah. I know."

Nicole's voice dropped another notch. "I missed last Christmas with her, 'cause I was so sick," she said. "I ain't ever going to let that happen again." She raised her eyes from her sleeping child to gaze at him. "You shouldn't ever do that. Not if you can help it."

He left them in the chapel and stepped into the office. Reverend Callum had relaxed in his old chair, his eyes closed and hands folded across his middle, at peace as he listened to the music from the radio.

Joe said, "Reverend?"

"I'm sorry I went to barking like that," the reverend murmured. "I don't know you. You're a good man, far as I can tell."

"Not good enough," Joe said.

"Well, who can't say that?" Callum opened his eyes and tilted his head to the chapel. "What about those two now?"

Joe said, "I'm going to take them home with me. To my house."

"That be all right with your family?"

"It'll be fine. They'll be welcome." The reverend looked dubious, but didn't comment further. Joe said, "I'm not trying to be noble, sir. Or make a point or anything."

Reverend Callum nodded. "Good. Nobody needs that." He pushed the telephone across the desk. "I guess you want to call a cab, then."

Joe said, "I was hoping we could take the van."

The reverend frowned. "Where'd you say you lived? By the college? That's a long drive up and back. It's late. And I'm tired."

Joe said, "Yes, sir, but I'm hoping you'll come, too. For Christmas morning. We'll have breakfast." He felt a catch in his throat. "It's a family tradition."

The music played softly from the radio. Reverend Callum seemed to be looking past Joe and at something in the distance. He said, "That's kind of you, but…"

"You have someplace to be?" The reverend shook his head. "Then I'd consider it a favor. And an honor."

Reverend Callum laughed quietly. "You show up with three strangers, three *black* strangers, and your wife's going to hit the roof. It's what, now, three in the morning?"

"She'll be fine. The kids, too." He tamped down the throb in his chest and found himself saying *please* again, and then, "I'd be grateful."

"It's a kind invitation," the reverend said.

Joe said, "So we can go now?"

It was time for the last act and Joe was ready to get on with it. He spent a minute sharing the plan with Nicole as Malikah dozed in her lap. When he finished, she treated him to a searching look.

"You sure it's all right?" she said.

"It's fine. The reverend's coming along."

She said, "I figured he would be."

Joe stepped out the door onto the snow-crusted sidewalk. Behind him, Malikah's voice was like a sleepy bell as she asked where they were going now. He was turning to answer her when he heard a loud crack followed by another and felt a blow and then a knifing pain in his left bicep. As he clutched his elbow, he heard the reverend shout something and Nicole shriek all raw and angry.

"What?" he said over the noise in his ears. "What's wrong?"

Nicole was yelling, "Goddamn you, Terry! Goddamn you!"

Now he felt a searing heat in his arm and he groped to find the sleeve of his coat soaked wet. In the next second, Reverend Callum whipped around him in a dark blur as he went to his knees on the cold concrete.

The first cruiser came wailing from Northampton Street with wild lights flashing. Joe, slouching against the storefront, shoved aside the impossible notion that he had been shot to consider that without the whooping of the sirens, the red and white and blue lights would be full of festive life.

Nicole had pulled his coat off one arm. She groaned when she saw his sweater wet with blood. She whipped off her scarf and wrapped it around the arm as far up as she could go and he grunted at the pain. But the bleeding stopped and the sharp ache settled into a throb.

In a breathless rush, she told him that Terry had fired twice. One bullet hit Joe's arm. The second had nicked Reverend Callum's right hand. Joe saw the reverend standing in the middle of the sidewalk with his foot planted on Terry's hollow chest and his hands clasped together as if in violent prayer. Nicole had ministered to him, too, wrapping a towel from the church bathroom around a wound to his palm.

"Where did he come from?" Joe asked her.

"He must have followed us from the house. Saw the van and…" Her voice trembled. "I'm so sorry. I can't believe he did this."

Watching her face, Joe's fog lifted a bit. "What about Malikah?"

"She's okay. She's inside."

"You left her alone with the cookies?" he said and saw sudden tears spring to the mother's eyes.

The sirens blared louder and in the next seconds, the first patrol car slid to the curb. Two officers leaped out, their weapons drawn and pointed upward. Stalking around the car to the sidewalk, they conducted an instant survey of the scene. One of them, a short black man with a lean build, seemed to know the reverend and asked him to stand away. In a flurry of rough motion, he and his partner cuffed Terry and jerked him to his feet. The second cop, white and as burly as a wrestler, hustled the suspect to the cruiser and bent him over the hood.

The black cop approached Joe, kneeled down, peered at his bloody sleeve, and stared into his face. "Thomas" was spelled out on the silver tag over his breast pocket.

He said, "Sir, are you all right?" Joe nodded. "The EMTs are on the way. What's your name?"

"Joe Kelly. Joseph."

"Do you have some ID, sir?"

Joe said, "Pocket."

Nicole fished until she found his wallet. She handed the policeman Joe's license and he flicked his minimag over it. "What happened here?" he said.

"I didn't see," Joe said.

The cop turned to Nicole. "Ma'am?"

She told him in a shaking voice how Joe had gone out the door ahead of her. She heard the two shots. The reverend shouted something and Joe folded to his knees. She saw Terry standing thirty feet down the walk with the pistol in his hand. She was dragging Malikah out of the way when Reverend Callum charged past her, knocked the weapon out of Terry's hand, and smacked him to the sidewalk.

Joe was awed. "He did that?"

She nodded. "Put him right down. Then stood on him."

Officer Thomas tilted his head to the cruiser and said, "And this individual. Mister..."

"Neal," Nicole said.

"Neal. He followed you here?"

"He lives down on Grant Street," she said. "That's where he came from."

The cop's eyes shifted back to Joe. "How do you know him, sir?"

Joe said, "I don't. Didn't. He put her and the kid out of the house. I was helping the reverend tonight and went to collect them."

"You were helping the reverend how?" Thomas said.

"I answered the phone for him."

The officer was about to ask another question when the clashing lights and sirens of a second and a third cruiser and a boxy ambulance cut him off. He told Joe he'd wait for the EMTs to work on him before taking the rest of his statement. He straightened and stepped back as the ambulance slid to the curb.

The EMT who jumped down from the passenger side looked too young, but was clearly the one in charge. Her hair was cut short and parted in the middle, and though she was all business, Joe liked her face. He guessed she was Italian and smiled when he saw the tag stitched on her jumpsuit: *Antonicci.* In two quick movements, she opened one of the side panels on the truck and pulled out a medical kit. The driver who stepped from the cab was in his thirties and reminded Joe of a soldier. They conferred with Officer Thomas, glancing over at Joe and Reverend

Callum. The driver grabbed a kit of his own and moved to tend to the reverend.

Officer Thomas and Antonicci kneeled down. The EMT nodded briefly to Nicole, glanced at Joe's face, then studied his arm. Joe regarded her in a daze. She had a nice face, olive-toned with freckles, a good nose, and very dark eyes.

She was all business. "Sir?" she said. "Can you get up and walk to the ambulance?"

Joe nodded and said, "Think so."

Officer Thomas and the EMT helped him to his feet. They stood still for a moment, then Antonicci fitted herself under his left arm and wrapped him around his waist, as if they were lovers embarking on a stroll. He felt like giggling as she managed him across the sidewalk toward the back of the ambulance.

Nicole said, "My daughter. She's inside."

Office Thomas said, "Go ahead, ma'am. Just don't leave the scene, please."

Joe and the EMT had gone only a few steps when he stopped.

"Wait a minute." He moved his good arm to pat his pockets in a clumsy way. "Where is it?"

"Where is what, sir?"

"It was in my pocket," Joe said. "A box."

The officer patted Joe's coat and then the front of his jeans. "What kind of box, sir?"

"Something I bought. I think I dropped it."

He tried to turn around but Antonicci was holding him fast. "We've got to get into the vehicle now."

Joe turned his head to call over his shoulder. "Nicole!" The movement made him dizzy and his legs went loose. The EMT lifted his foot onto the metal step and she and the cop hoisted him into the vehicle. Antonicci peeled off Joe's coat and then his sweater and shirt. After cleaning the wound with a solution that shot shards of pain through his arm, she bound it with a bandage and draped a blanket over his exposed side. She explained that he had suffered a gunshot wound to his bicep. That part he knew. "It was a small caliber," she said. "A .22 or a .25. The bullet passed through the back without striking the bone, so the damage is all to tissue. But you're going to require treatment at the ER. We'll be transporting you in a few minutes."

"Transporting me where?"

"Charity."

Joe said, "Shot?" He was back to being stunned by the news.

Antonicci peered more closely. "Is there anyone

you want to call?"

Joe thought about it. He shook his head. "Not now. Later."

The EMT gave the bandages another inspection, then told him they'd be leaving directly and made her way back to the cab.

After a few numb seconds, a film began rolling in his head. First came the blunt, sudden shock, followed by the bolt of pain. The sidewalk tilts and he's on his knees, staring at the dark stain seeping through the fabric of his coat. In the next instant, he turns his head to see Terry standing twenty feet away, a shaking wreck, the pistol dangling from his hand. Reverend Callum appears from out of the frame moving with an agility that's amazing for such a large man, grabs Terry's wrist, twists the weapon away, then slaps him to the ground with a thick palm. Only after he kicks the pistol down the sidewalk and plants one large shoe on Terry's chest does he clutch his own bloody left hand. Nicole is kneeling at his side, her eyes wild, wailing, *Oh, my God! What should I do? What should I do?* Joe says: *My cell phone. 911.* And she fumbles into his coat pockets until she finds it and starts punching numbers. He looks past her to see Malikah gaping in wonder at his arm, her mouth a

THE NIGHT BEFORE

wide O as the projector winds down and stops.

A magazine article he had read came to mind. It was a story about movie deals falling through because the incidents they were based on were so improbable that no one would believe something that crazy could have happened. Now he understood.

Officer Thomas reappeared, clipboard in hand. He climbed into the ambulance, sat down on the opposite bench, and spent a few minutes letting Joe walk him through the crime, starting with the call to the church and ending with the reverend slapping Terry to the ground. The cop closed his clipboard and told Joe to expect to be contacted about a court date. He called up to Antonicci that he was finished and with a perfunctory nod, stepped down. In the next moment, Nicole climbed inside and handed Joe the zebrawood box. He sighed with relief and clutched it tight.

She went back to tend to Malikah and Reverend Callum appeared at the ambulance door. "How are you feeling, son?"

"I'm all right," Joe said. "How about you?"

The reverend flipped his bandaged hand. "This ain't nothing," he said. "Just barely got me."

Nicole and Malikah sidled up next to him and peered inside. Behind them, the car with Terry in the back seat pulled out, blue lights flashing in the darkness.

"You taking him to Charity?" the reverend called to Antonicci.

"Yes, sir," the EMT said. "We'll be leaving in just a second."

"We'll follow you, then." He smiled at Joe. "You know, we're both lucky it wasn't worse. Boy would have pointed that pistol an inch or two left or right and..." He lifted his arms and said, "I guess God had other plans for us tonight."

Joe stared at Reverend Callum's retreating back. He was still working to get his mind around the reverend's parting words when the male EMT stepped up to strap him to the steel cot and then join Antonicci in the cab.

By the time they reached the hospital, Joe was wondering frankly if he had been transported into someone else's movie after all. Never one to shy away from trouble, he had never hidden behind his computer and then pretended to know life's raw realities. He had worked blue-collar jobs, construction and such, and had always felt more at home on the funkier side of a street. It was yet another point on which he and Mariel diverged, but he believed his books were the better for it and so did the critics who had reviewed them. He was not afraid to get his hands dirty, get into it, *engage*.

But this night was beyond ridiculous. If it wasn't for the hole in his arm, the stricken looks on the faces of Nicole and Malikah, and the gleaming display of steel, glass, and plastic apparatus around him, it could have been a silly dream, a plot line he made up and then discarded.

The ER nurse, a brisk and cheerful Latina, escorted him to a gurney and then closed the curtain. He sat there for a little while, trying to piece together the fragments of the last ten hours and wondering if it would ever make sense. Heroes got shot, but he didn't feel like a hero. Mariel and Christian would be distraught when they found out. He hoped Hannah wouldn't think it had been a thrilling adventure. Maybe the reality of his wound would shock her out of such notions. He could only hope.

The curtain opened and the nurse was back with a doctor who looked like a gawky kid. He asked Joe some general questions and his condition. Neither he nor the nurse was all that excited about his wound, just another entry in a catalog of damaged body parts.

In what seemed a matter of a few busy seconds, the doctor had cleansed and stitched his flesh and the nurse had re-bandaged and wrapped and taped his bicep. The doctor wrote out some prescriptions and now it was the nurse asking Joe if there was anyone he wanted to contact.

Joe thought it over and pictured Mariel answering the phone in the middle of her frenetic night to hear him babbling a story about getting shot and going to the hospital. She'd think he'd lost his mind. Also, there was the chance that she wouldn't pick up, fearing what she might hear. He shook his head. "My friends are outside."

The nurse said, "All right, then. Someone's coming in to get your insurance information and all that." Joe made a face and she said, "I know. But as soon as she's done, you can go."

"Okay," Joe said. He was noticing how nicely her curves filled her scrubs. Maybe he wasn't in such bad shape after all.

When she pulled back the curtain, Joe saw Reverend Callum, Nicole, and Malikah waiting. The reverend's hand had been bandaged so that he looked like a boxer in wraps. Nicole stepped to Joe's side while the reverend settled in the chair. There was nothing gory for Malikah to witness so she contented herself with studying all the shiny medical gear. However the shooting had alarmed her, she wasn't showing any signs. Nicole appeared far more shaken over what had transpired.

Joe asked what time it was, then said, "You're still coming to the house, right?"

The reverend and Nicole exchanged a glance.

Reverend Callum said, "We can carry you there, but we weren't sure…"

"What?"

"That it'd be right. With what happened and all."

"Doesn't matter," Joe said.

Malikah piped up. "I want to go."

Joe nodded. "I'd say that settles it."

The reverend said, "We'll talk about it once we get you out of here."

Joe was on his way to insisting when a woman in slacks and a white blouse approached on quick clicking heels, pushing a laptop cart. She introduced herself as Ms. Tolliver from Accounting. From her curt voice and the pinched way she peered at the computer screen, she was not happy about having to work the holiday. It didn't seem to occur to her that no one else wanted to be there, either.

Joe asked Nicole to go into his pocket for his wallet and dig out his insurance card. Ms. Tolliver used the mobile stand to copy his information.

"This is the policy from your wife's employer?" she asked.

Joe felt his face reddening. "That's right."

The woman typed in the account number from the card and hit a few more keys. Peering over the top of the screen, she said, "Mr. Callum?"

"It's 'Reverend,'" Joe said.

"I'm sorry. Reverend. Do you have insurance coverage, sir?"

"I'm a veteran. I go to the VA."

"Yes, sir, I understand. However, there's going to be a charge for the EMT treating the wound at the scene. And some Emergency Room charges. What arrangements —"

"Hey!" It came out sharper than Joe had intended and the woman stopped, frowned, and hiked her eyebrows. "How much?" he said.

Ms. Tolliver's lips pursed. "I don't have the exact final to—"

"Okay, about how much?"

"About... eighteen hundred dollars," the woman said.

The reverend held up his bandaged hand, appalled. "For this?"

Joe said, "I'll cover it." As the three adults and the child stared, he bent down and retrieved the sheaf of bills from his sock. He passed the stack to Nicole. "Count out two thousand."

The reverend said, "Mister Joe, I can —"

"It's not charity," Joe said quickly. "I want to do it."

It was true; the woman's tone had set him off. Reverend Callum leaned forward to speak, then stopped when Joe shook his head. Joe watched as Nicole dropped one C-note after another onto Ms. Tolliver's keyboard. The woman's grimace of distaste deepened. Too bad for her; Joe was in no mood to be civil.

"Okay, let's go," he said when Nicole had delivered the last bill.

She helped him with his jacket and she and the reverend started for the door.

Ms. Tolliver said, "Wait, please. I'm printing a receipt."

Joe stood by while the paper rattled out of the printer that was perched on the shelf below the laptop. Ms. Tolliver handed him the page. "If you're due a refund, you can —"

"He's a man of God," Joe told her tight face. "And a veteran." He walked away.

Reverend Callum and Nicole were waiting by the ER door.

"You didn't need to do that," the reverend said. "I got money."

"I wanted to," Joe repeated. "And I could." The reverend treated him to a baffled look. "It's all right. I'll explain it later."

Nicole called, "Malikah?" The child had disappeared.

Nicole called out again. "Malikah!"

The adults stepped into the corridor and circled the floor, arriving back where they began. Nicole was starting to get frantic and Joe had just asked a nurse to call security when she noticed the directory on the wall. She peered at it for a few moments, then said, "It's okay. I know where she went."

She stood at the bright window, peering wide-eyed at the half-dozen tiny bodies in their bassinets. Joe caught up with Nicole at the top of the stairs and they stood in silence in the doorway, watching Malikah as she pressed her nose to the glass. Joe stole a glance at Nicole and saw something sad and unreadable in her eyes.

"How'd you know she'd be here?"

"I just figured…" There was more to it, but he didn't press. After a few moments, she said, "She's looking for her little brother."

"What little brother?"

"The one we lost."

She moved off. Joe watched as she slipped next to her daughter and bent down. Together, mother and child gazed in at the newborns. Then Nicole put her arm around Malikah's shoulder and murmured, "It's time to go."

Reverend Callum drove with Joe giving directions. Malikah was asleep with her head in her mother's lap. The city was quiet under the blanket of snow and a pre-dawn sky the color of slate.

Joe asked the reverend to retrace his path through the night, driving past the church and through the neighborhoods. Jimmy's was closed and he peered along Queen Street, where Gina and Sonny were nestled. He thought about rousing them to come along to the house. And what about Billy and the friend that he had surely found? The more the merrier. No, let them all huddle in warm beds. For this night and a thousand more, if they could manage it.

The reverend interrupted his thoughts. "You don't think you should maybe call ahead?" he said.

Joe said, "That would just get everybody excited. It's better this way."

"I don't remember when's the last time I was in a home on Christmas morning," the reverend said. "With the church and all, I don't get to."

"Where are your people?" Joe said, feeling the sweet respite of talking about common matters.

"In Georgia," Callum murmured. "What's left of them, I mean. They're all mostly gone." He fell silent, leaving only the sound of the hum of the engine, the whirr of the heater fan, and the tires rolling on the packed snow. Another few moments and he said, "I had a wife and children. They're gone, too."

"Gone where?" Nicole said.

Reverend Callum didn't speak for several seconds and Joe wondered if they had stumbled onto something tragic.

"The whiskey bottle," the reverend said at last. "That was how the devil got hold of me. I was weak. Couldn't fight him. And so he won out. They up and left me. Moved away. I don't know where." It had all come out in a deep and measured voice, like slow-running water. "I imagine my little girl has her own family by now." He smiled in a distant way. "Means I'm a granddaddy. Or so I expect."

"You don't want to track them down?" Joe said.

Reverend Callum was quiet for another few moments before saying, "I will someday. Yes, I will." They passed under Highway 12 and turned onto College Avenue. "Don't get up this way much," the reverend murmured.

Joe said, "I can help you. Find your people, I mean. I know how to do research. I have to do it for my books."

"What books?" the reverend said.

"I write books. That's what I do. For a living."

"Is that so?" The reverend's brow stitched as he watched the road. "I never asked you, did I?"

"What kind of books?" Nicole said.

Joe turned in his seat. "Novels. Historical." He felt as if he was confessing to something. "So I do a lot of research." He looked at the reverend again. "I could help. If you wanted to find someone, I mean."

The reverend met his eyes, then returned his attention to the road. "Well, maybe…"

"You in the bookstores?" Nicole said.

"I have been, yeah." Joe felt himself blushing again, though now with pride. "And I will be again soon."

Nicole eyed him. "So what's your next one about?"

"My next one?" Joe felt a fresh throb in his arm. "I don't know. Maybe about tonight."

"That'd be some story, all right," the reverend said.

He directed Reverend Callum onto his street. As the van rolled up to the house, Joe saw Don whisking away with a heavy broom at the patches of drifted snow that had sullied his driveway.

The reverend shut off the engine. Don stopped and stared wide-eyed as the three adults and the child piled out. By the time he discerned that one of the passengers was Joe, it was too late to make a run for it. So he stood still, broom in hand, his face blanching from winter-morning red to a sickly white that was clear even at that distance.

Nicole glanced his way. "Jesus," she said under her breath. "Him?"

Joe bent to retrieve the spare key from beneath a flagstone. "Yeah. Him."

"I guess ugly ain't against the law," she said, causing Joe to cough.

Don stood frozen in a fearful sort of wonder, and whatever dreams of violence Joe had been entertaining dwindled away. He couldn't muster the passion to fix

THE NIGHT BEFORE

him with as much as a vile glance as they made their way up the walk. No one looked at Don anymore and he was a snowman melting into a greasy puddle of his own making.

It was not until the middle of the night that Mariel fell into a sleep that was assailed by odd and disjointed dreams. She jerked awake, dozed, then came alert again. Twice she felt her stomach churning so roughly that she thought she'd have to run to the bathroom, but both times the spasms passed and she sat on the edge of the bed, her dull eyes fixed on the floor while she waited for her nerves to calm.

As the hours wore on, her fears that something had gone wrong with Joe ran wild. He wouldn't stay away from his kids that long, not him, and not at Christmas. He wouldn't hurt them because of her treachery. He was a good man that way.

Who was she kidding? He was a good man in most ways. His poor earning potential wasn't a crime. She had known about his slapdash nature all along, starting with their very first months together. He dreamed and chased rainbows and left the worries over money to her.

She knew that he possessed a remarkable talent,

that he worked very hard, that his books were accomplished. All that and a dollar-fifty would get him a ride on the #6 bus. It was something he repeated when things were slow, which was most of the time. But his negligence didn't make him a felon. Or worthy of betrayal.

Her fears for his safety rose to her throat with a sour taste. To escape from the dark and crazy thoughts that were crossing her mind, she spent some time recalling certain moments: the first time she had seen him as a student in a writing class he was teaching; their first kiss and the first time they had lain together; when the children were born, Christian in the bright of late morning and Hannah at midnight, as their natures dictated. She wondered what time of day Joe had been born. Had she ever asked him? She couldn't remember, but she guessed it was in the kind shadows of a quiet dawn just like this one.

She rested her head on the pillow, thinking that there were other sweet shreds that she should have grabbed onto, a word or a look that told her that the moment was special. But too many times, she had just let it slip by, instead fuming because he couldn't be more sensible. This was her failing.

She didn't realize that she had drifted back to sleep

THE NIGHT BEFORE

until the odd noises woke her, the clanking chassis and stuttering engine of a lone vehicle rolling up the street and coming to a creaking stop at the end of their drive. She pushed herself out of bed in the gray light and peeked through the curtain.

A battered van with a scroll of letters painted on the side sat at the curb. As she watched, the engine quieted, the side door slid wide, and a thin black woman climbed down, followed by a little girl bundled in a coat that was too big for her. A burly bearded man, also black, appeared from behind the wheel and made his way to the sidewalk, moving with a pronounced dignity. She noticed that his left hand was bandaged.

She choked out a sob, sensing before she saw him that Joe was in the van. Who else could it be? When the passenger door opened and he climbed down from the seat, she saw the sling that held his arm and let out a sharp sigh. Hadn't she known something was wrong? Now she watched as he stopped to stare in a flat way in the direction of the garage next door and noticed for the first time the sound of shoveling or sweeping. Don was out working on his driveway. On Christmas morning.

She waited to see if Joe was going to say or do

anything, ready for whatever happened. But he and his companions started up the walk at what seemed a weary pace. He did not raise his eyes.

The house was quiet and everything in the main room was familiar to Joe's eye: the sturdy, earthy furniture, the paintings and photographs on the walls, the tree lit up and dazzling in the corner. And yet it felt like a place he had left some time ago. He knew that this was common among people who had endured a profound shock. Their worlds were jogged so far sideways that much of what they knew seemed for a short while brand new.

Though thrilled at the sight of the tree, Malikah was still sleepy and Nicole asked if she could put her down for a little while. Joe helped get her situated under a blanket on the couch, then invited Nicole and the reverend into the kitchen. Reverend Callum settled at the table with a sigh of comfort. When Joe tried making coffee with his one good hand, Nicole nudged him aside and took over.

He joined the reverend at the table. His thoughts turned to the kids and he realized that he hadn't heard any sounds from the house. He wondered if Mariel had taken them to her parents' house in Nazareth or to her sister's in Jersey. As if in reply, footsteps thumped in the upstairs hall, followed by the bathroom door closing and water running in the pipes.

"Nice table you got here." The reverend laid his good hand on the surface. "You build it yourself?"

"Years ago." Joe smiled curiously. "How did you know?"

"It has that look."

"That bad?"

Reverend Callum shook his head. "No, no, you did good. It just don't look manufactured, that's all." He told Joe that he did some woodwork himself. Yes, he had cobbled the rough cross that hung in the chapel. He was describing how he had gone about hewing the cedar by hand when he stopped to stare at something. In the same instant, Joe sensed that Nicole had gone still.

He turned in his chair to see Mariel standing in the doorway. Their eyes met and he felt a hollow pang in the pit of his stomach. She blinked and bit her lip, then shifted her gaze to the strangers: the black man at the table with his bandaged hand and the woman leaning against the sideboard, her arms crossed and ebony eyes narrowed, which meant she knew.

She started to speak, then lost her way, and Joe said, "Mariel, this is Reverend Callum and Nicole. That's her daughter Malikah on the couch. They're joining us for Christmas morning."

Mariel gazed between the reverend and Nicole and managed a weak smile.

Joe said, "They still asleep?"

"Yes." She appeared befuddled, her face drained of color and her eyes cloudy and Joe tried to imagine what was going through her head. Then he thought about how many times a sad little drama like theirs played out in kitchens and living rooms and bedrooms, everywhere and forever.

She fixed her gaze on the sling. "Your arm," she said. "What happened to your arm?"

Joe said, "Oh. There was a... an incident."

Mariel stared, baffled. "A what?"

"This guy had a gun and he —"

"A gun?" Her eyes widened. "You were shot?"

"The reverend was hit, too," Joe said. "In the hand."

She gasped and blinked at her tears. She said, "Oh, my God, Joe..."

"It's okay," he said. "We were lucky."

"Shot by who?"

THE NIGHT BEFORE

Nicole spoke up. "Man I've been seeing. He has a drug problem. Joe was helping me and he came with a gun."

Mariel said, "How did…" She couldn't find the words and said, "Shot?" again and stared at her husband as if he was some ragged soul who had wandered all bloodied into her house with a stray trio of street people, maybe characters he had created for one of his books and had somehow brought to life.

"Excuse me," Nicole said. "How do y'all take your coffee?"

When Mariel edged out of the kitchen, Joe got up and followed her. The lack of sleep, the jumble of the night's events, and the pain that was invading his arm and shoulder had him punchy, and he had to measure his steps. But when he stepped into his office in the back of the house, he relaxed, slipping into a cocoon of his own making. The room was his private little universe and Mariel had always been kind about leaving it alone. Now he stood by his desk and surveyed the happy mess while she clung to the wall next to the door.

He gazed out his window at a distant ridge that dusted white with snow, and thought about the years he had spent there, working away mostly in solitude, tapping out dreams as his wife and children moved through their lives. And now they had arrived... where? He had gone through a dark adventure and returned with a magical amulet and a piece of paper that proved his work was by someone's lights worthy. Yet he couldn't say what it any of it meant.

Mariel broke into these meandering thoughts. "My God." She was back to staring at the sling.

"I was lucky," Joe repeated. "We were. We are."

She rubbed her arms and shuddered. "What happened to the man?"

"The police took him away. I'll have to go testify."

"How did you meet the... your friends?"

Joe said, "Another time, Mariel. It's been a long night."

She said, "You can't tell me what happened? How you almost got yourself killed?"

"No, I can't. Not now."

When he turned away his eyes came to rest on the shelf that held the copies of his three books. They appeared to him as orphans who had been lost and now were found. He realized that he had yet to tell Mariel about the option. Maybe it was childish, but he had earned the privilege of his secret, had bled for it, in fact, and decided to hold it as a bit of armor over his wounds. He indulged an inward smile as he stopped to ponder where he would be without drama.

He sighed as the unspoken pushed these notions aside. "So," he said. "Was it worth it?"

Mariel shook her head. "No."

He could tell by the broken look on her face that she was prepared to stand there and let him take his shots. Because other than a decade of failure, she had nothing on him, no defense for her actions. Her guns were empty.

"So why'd you do it? And why with him?"

She considered, looking miserable. "Because I... I thought I wanted... I was feeling..." She trailed off and ran a shaky hand over her face, wiping away a tear.

"Feeling what?" Joe said.

Mariel said, "Like I was carrying you and the kids." She gestured to the air. "The house. Our lives. And that it was going to be like that forever."

Joe dropped his voice. "And the way you dealt with it was to do the next-door neighbor on our dining room table?"

Mariel's chin took a set. "That's what I did, yes."

"The guy is a fucking weasel."

"Yeah, you would think that. You and Billy."

Joe cocked an eyebrow, surprised. "What does he have to do with this?"

"Nothing. Nothing at all." After an agonized pause, she said, "You're right. He is a weasel. I know." So they agreed on that. "So now what?" she said.

Joe didn't know what to say and wondered if it mattered. It was done. There was no erasing it, no going back for a rewrite. The woman he had courted and married and with whom he had made two fine children had vacated the premises, leaving an enfeebled stranger stretched against the wall, with no idea of what the coming days would bring and hoping for but not expecting mercy. He understood that no small something had been taken out of her, too. He wished that she had considered that before she leaped into Don Banks' embrace.

He heard the reverend's gentle laugh from the kitchen and perked an ear, longing to be in the light and warmth of the room with those two good people. Meanwhile, his marriage seemed to be passing like a slow-moving train on its way to nowhere. He was mulling this notion when a new twinge of pain shot up his arm. The medication was wearing off and the pain went deeper.

"So what do I tell the kids?" he said.

Mariel treated him to a fretful look. "Can't it wait?"

"I mean about this," he said, raising his slung arm.

"Oh. The truth, I guess." She smiled faintly. "Hannah will think it's the coolest thing you've ever done."

"And what about…"

She stared at the floor. "You decide what happens next. It's only fair. But not now. Not today."

Joe said. "I wouldn't do that." He took a final look out the window at the white fields and the hills beyond. "It's Christmas morning."

He crossed to the door. As he passed, Mariel reached out a hand, then caught herself and let it drop, a falling leaf of regret.

He found his guests at the table, relaxed over their steaming cups. The reverend regarded him with interest as he took a chair. Nicole got up to warm his coffee and hiked a questioning eyebrow when she placed it before him.

"It's all right," he said. "It's fine." He sipped the brew and found it delicious. How could he have forgotten how good coffee could taste? Or the way the morning sunlight the color of clover honey could drench a room? Or that sometimes something sweet was submerged even in bitter waters?

They chatted about nothing. At one point, Joe heard a flurried slamming of car doors and got up to peer out the front window in time to see Don's SUV wheel into the street and race away. That the man had rousted his family and bolted to grandmother's house or wherever gave him a moment's satisfaction. Though he felt bad for the kid.

No, he didn't. He wondered if in the next days he could expect to see a For Sale sign popping out of the snow that covered the Banks' front yard.

He finished his coffee and trekked through the snow to reclaim the Saab while Nicole fetched her stash of gifts from the van. Once they got back and started spreading the boxes under the tree, he realized that he had indeed bought too much, and so he assigned some of the overage to Malikah and left the rest in the car.

He didn't know what to do about Mariel. He didn't want to look at or talk to her. She lingered on the periphery of his vision in a way that made him feel that she had stepped out of his world.

They were applying the last touches when he glanced at Nicole and saw her gazing into the kitchen with a strange light in her eyes. He moved to her side and peered through the doorway to see Mariel and the reverend at the table. Mariel's palms covered her eyes and her cheeks were streaked with tears. The reverend's hands were joined before him and his eyes were dark pools as he murmured in a voice so low that Joe couldn't hear.

Nicole watched them for another moment, then patted Joe's shoulder in a kind way and went back to work.

He heard footsteps along the second floor hallway. He had just reached the bottom of the stairwell when he heard Hannah's voice. When her pretty freckled face poked around the corner at the top of the stairs, he felt his heart rise into his throat and his legs go weak.

"Daddy?" She padded down the steps in her sleepwear as he climbed to meet her. She stopped, her eyes going wide at the sight of the sling. "What happened to you?"

"I'll tell you later," Joe said and drew her into the circle of his good arm. In the next moment, her brother appeared and he had to bite down to keep from weeping.

Christian looked over his shoulder at the figure on

the couch. "Who's that?"

Joe found his voice. "It's Christmas," he said. "And we have company."

The kids attacked the boxes while the adults watched them, sipped coffee, and pondered their private Christmas morning thoughts.

As Joe watched them and saw their faces full of such joy, he imagined that it had been a dream: he had not caught his wife in that vulgar embrace with a creep of a neighbor; he had not stumbled upon a face from the past; he had not been mugged on a snowy street and rescued by a kind preacher; and had not tried to help a mother and child, only to take a bullet through the arm for his trouble.

And now, as he sat safely enclosed in his armchair, he wondered if he would be able to tell the story of what had transpired over the night and morning. An urge to get up and hurry to his office and begin tapping out the words assailed him. Then he looked around the room and decided that it could wait. There would be time. There would be time for that, for his children, for his friends.

Whatever was going to become of him and Mariel would wait, too. There would be time for everything that mattered.

The packages were unwrapped and each child put one aside to be donated to someone in need. It was something they did every holiday. The crumpled bright paper was stashed into a leaf bag that leaned in the corner. Mariel still hadn't met his eyes. She wore the face of a penitent, pale and suffering. The kids pretended not to notice.

She stood up, looking out of place in her own home. "I should start breakfast," she said and moved toward the kitchen.

Joe caught Nicole's pointed stare. "Wait, please," he said.

Mariel stopped to watch with the others as he reached into his pocket for the zebrawood box. When he drew out the pendant by the thin chain and held it up to the light, he barely caught the soft sob that trebled her throat.

Hannah said, "What is it?"

"It's called an Epiphany Star," the reverend said. "Ain't that right, Mister Joe?"

Christian said, "Who's it for?"

Joe thought for a few seconds, then said, "It's for all of us."

He found a place on the mantle to drape it. The

jewels caught the tree lights and the morning sun and cast out different colored rays as it twisted slowly on its chain. Joe turned around to find Mariel staring at the pendant with an expression he couldn't read.

He nudged her with a gentle voice. "Breakfast?" Her gaze found him and she started to say something, but couldn't find the words.

The children were back to chattering over their gifts as the adults made their way to the kitchen. Nicole leaned close to Joe and whispered, "Aren't you forgetting something?"

It was then that he remembered that he still had the folded letter and the bank slip in his pocket.

"Tomorrow," he said.

THE END

About the Author

David Fulmer has been a finalist for the LA Times Book Prize and won the Shamus Award for Best First Novel. He lives in Atlanta. Visit davidfulmer.com.